Guitar Hero

Day's Lee

Guitar Hero is a work of fiction. Names, characters, places and incidents are either the product of the author's imagination or used fictitiously. Any resemblance to actual events or persons, living or dead, is entirely coincidental.

Cover illustration by Robin Patterson
Copy editing by Virginia Modugno

ISBN-13: 978-1482358247
ISBN-10: 1482358247

DEDICATION

For Davin, Emma and Matthew

ACKNOWLEDGMENTS

The support and encouragement of family and friends helped me through the process of writing, this, my first novel. In particular, I would like to thank Monique Polak and Lori Weber for encouraging me to turn the original short story into a novel, my critique group, Virginia Modugno, Robin Patterson, Alastair Reeves, Judie Troyansky, and Helen Wolkowicz for reading the manuscript in various stages, James Morehouse and Collin Steinz for their musical guidance, and Sebastien Hébert of the Queen Elizabeth Hotel. I would also like to thank Maggie Jagger, Michael Ferguson, Sandy Chan, Jesse Douglas, Leah Douglas, Amanda Lee-Roy, Kim Lo and Jennifer Hong. Any mistakes are my own.

CHAPTER 1

The worst things happen in the dead of the night.

It's almost midnight when I hear the front door open. My dad's finally home. He's only six hours late this time. The low murmur of the late-night news snaps off. For a few moments there's an eerie silence, like in a horror movie before the axe falls. In this case, the axe is my mom. She stayed up waiting for him to come home, mentally sharpening her blade.

Snatches of words and phrases in Chinese, low and harsh, creep up the stairs. Sounding angry and scared, my mother throws out words like "debt" and "house payment". My dad's quiet apologies interrupt her.

Lately they've been fighting about money as often as a radio station plays a Top Ten hit. Last year, my dad lost his job when the clothing company where he was assistant manager for over twenty years moved its operations to China. A few months ago, he got a job working the stockroom at a grocery store for minimum wage, less than half what he was making before.

I lie in bed, in the dark, practicing chords on my unplugged guitar. Street lamp glow streams through the open blinds, casting strips of light on the bedroom wall.

For weeks, I've been practicing day and night, until my fingertips are numb.

Because I'm playing with Pumping Iron this Saturday in the Montreal Rocks Contest!

My best friend, Craig Chemielewski, formed Pumping Iron with a few other guys from school. They've been practicing together for about a year. I even wrote a couple of songs for them. Craig writes the music and I write the lyrics. We're Chang and Chemielewski, and we're going to be the Lennon and McCartney of our generation.

A couple of the other guys weren't too thrilled when Craig suggested that since I was writing for the band, they should give me the chance to play with them. Mick especially. He's such a diva. I don't want to give Mick a reason to kick me out, so I'm happy playing backup.

I finger the strings, listening carefully to the quiet notes. "Hey, John," I whisper to the black and white poster of The Beatles on the wall. "How's this?" I play the chord. He doesn't say it sucks.

I've been taking guitar lessons every Saturday for the past few months. It looked so cool to be in a band that I had to try. Once I got started, I was hooked. Mark, my teacher, told me that I have talent. "The music's inside you. You have to keep practicing to draw it out." I practice so much that Mom says the guitar is permanently attached to my hip. I strum *Let It Be,* whispering the words as my parents bring their fight upstairs to their bedroom.

"David!" my dad shouts. "Put away that damn guitar and go to bed!"

It's not the first time he's said that, and it won't be the last.

I wait until their bedroom door slams shut, muffling their words. I can still hear the angry tone in Mom's voice. After a few seconds, when I'm sure they're too involved in their argument to notice, I continue where I left off and sing quietly to the end of the song. Then I lean the guitar against the wall beside the bed and lie down. It's time for the big performance with Bono. He's been begging me to play with Edge and the boys. Tonight, he gets his wish. Santana's just going to have to wait.

With my trusty air guitar, I play a solo that blows away audiences around the world. At least until I fall asleep. I know what'll happen in the morning: we'll all pretend we didn't hear them fight.

Sure enough, when I come down the next morning, Kim, my nine-year-old sister, is sitting at the kitchen table eating toast and telling my grandmother the latest gossip about her classmates. Dad's hiding behind the local Chinese newspaper. All I can see of him is the top of his thick black hair over the paper's edge. My mother stayed in bed, under the blankets. She prefers to cry when she's alone.

"Angela says her mother puts stuff into her lips with a needle so she won't look old." Kim licks jam off her fingers. "And Michael says his mother never tells anyone how old she is. But she's forty."

"Spilling everyone's secrets again?" I ask.

"It's only a secret from everyone in *school*," Kim points out.

"Old is good," Grandma says, in Chinese. "I am eighty-four years old. One becomes wiser with age." Although she's lived in Montreal for most of her adult life, she can barely speak English. Toishan is our dialect. Like every morning, she's busy packing leftovers for our lunch. I take a quick peek. Barbecue pork sandwiches and dried mango. All right!

When Yeh-yeh, our grandfather, passed away a few years ago, my parents decided Nai-nai, as Kim and I call her, would live with us. Nai-nai smells like the tiger balm she rubs on her legs every night to relieve her aching muscles. She's almost five feet, just tall enough to reach my armpits. Even though she's small, it's easy to pick her out in a crowd because she likes clothes with bright colors and patterns. Nothing matches, but we don't tell her. The yellow butterfly clip I gave her for Mother's Day last year keeps her white hair from falling into her face.

Long before I was born, Yeh-yeh and Nai-nai owned a Chinese hand laundry that was one of the last in Montreal to close. We have an old black-and-white photo of Yeh-yeh standing in the doorway of his new business, with a big smile on his face. He was young and skinny when he opened Chang's Chinese Hand Laundry. The words are hand-painted on a wooden sign over the door. It was sweaty, back-breaking work that left his hands red and raw.

Nai-nai left China when she was a teenager. She and her parents walked miles and miles, crossing a river to get to Hong Kong to look for a better life. After the Second World War, relatives arranged for her marriage to Yeh-yeh. After about a year, Yeh-yeh had to return to Canada, so they were separated until the Canadian government finally allowed Chinese men to bring their wives over. Uncle George was born first, then Dad, who's tall and lean like Grandpa was, with a full head of hair that I'm hoping is genetic.

I pour some Cheerios and milk into a bowl, then sit at the table to eat. My dad hasn't budged from behind the paper. The front page has a big picture of the prime minister and columns of Chinese characters. Sometimes I think it would be neat to know how to read Chinese, but Chinese school is on Saturdays, the same time as my guitar lessons. I have my priorities, and besides, I have all the homework I can handle.

"How come you came home so late?" I take a spoonful of cereal. The crunch fills up the sudden silence in the kitchen.

The pages stop moving, so I know he heard me, but he doesn't answer right away. "I was visiting some friends."

"The guy who runs mah-jongg games in the basement?"

The newspaper comes down a couple of inches. "How do you know that?"

I shrug. "Everyone knows. Why'd you go? I heard people there play for big money. You don't gamble."

Nai-nai nods in agreement. "Lim *Tai* knows someone's husband who gambled away the family business," she says in Chinese. Giving him a look that only a mother could, she continues, "Then they lost their house because they couldn't pay the mortgage. When the wife threatened to take the children and leave him, the husband tried to commit suicide. They live with some relatives now."

Kim's listening, wide-eyed.

The paper wall comes down. "What were you doing, playing guitar so late?" he says to me, ignoring Nai-nai.

"Just practicing."

"You should be studying."

"At least I was home," I reply, looking him in the eye.

He looks annoyed, tries to get the last word. "You better make sure you pass, or you won't graduate."

But I can't let him have it. "No problem. I got good marks. I could probably calculate the odds of you winning back the money."

The paper wall goes back up.

CHAPTER 2

There are two things I like about the month of May: one is that school's almost over, and the other is that the days are longer. More daylight means more freedom. My parents want me home by the time it gets dark, and in the winter, that means I barely have time to stick my foot in the front door before dusk falls.

At supper, I wolf down a few pieces of steamed chicken, Chinese broccoli, and a bowl of rice as if I haven't eaten all day.

"Why are you in such a hurry?" Kim lifts her bowl and pushes rice into her mouth with chopsticks.

"I'm going to Craig's," I say, and stuff another piece of chicken in my mouth.

Nai-nai looks pleased that I'm devouring her cooking. "My chicken tastes good," she says proudly. "Better than the one you bring home from the grocery store."

My parents nod in agreement. "You always make the best chicken," my dad replies with a smile. Then he looks at me. "Did you finish your homework?" He's always asking about homework. Ever since I was in fifth grade, he's made it clear that he expects me to go to university.

"All done," I say, suddenly remembering the book

6

report on Margaret Atwood due the day after tomorrow. "We're reviewing in class now anyway."

He frowns, but doesn't say anything.

"What're you going to do at Craig's?" my mom asks.

I shrug. "Just getting together with the guys." It's true, but I don't want to say why I'm going because they'll disapprove. Their lectures about finding a good job are getting old. My dad regrets dropping out of university. I mean it when I say I want to go, it's just that their idea of a good job and what I want to do aren't the same. Craig's parents support his dream one hundred percent. My parents are scared I'll ruin my life.

"Make sure you get home before dark." My dad jabs the air with his chopsticks to make his point. I think he should follow his own rule, but I don't say anything. Instead, I gulp down some Chinese tea, run up to my room for my guitar, and then I'm out of the house.

It only takes me a few minutes to get to Craig's. His house is a couple of blocks over, on a dead-end street, which makes it convenient for what we're going to do. As I head towards the brick house, I see the guys in the garage.

"Hey, dude!" Craig calls out as I'm walking up the driveway. He's sitting at the drums and looks ready to go. "You're gonna have to play lead until Andrew gets here. He's gonna be late."

"Cool!" I quickly slip my guitar out of the case and plug it into the amplifier.

Mick, busy setting up his keyboard, acknowledges me with a grunt. He's wearing his usual bad-boy outfit: tight black T-shirt with the sleeves rolled up to show off his muscles, worn-out jeans, and Converse running shoes. Todd stops tuning his bass guitar long enough to say, "Hey!" He always looks like he walked out of a Tommy Hilfiger ad. Mick and Todd are like yin and yang; completely opposite, but at the same time they complement each other. But I'd never say that out loud.

They're not exactly best friends.

For the Montreal Rocks Contest on Saturday, bands have to play both a cover and an original song. I love classic rock 'n' roll, and so does my guitar teacher. When I told Mark what we have to do, he helped me practice.

"Let's get started," says Todd. He turns to Craig, who's adjusting the mike. "How about we skip the vocals for now, so we can make sure we've got the chords down?"

"Sure," says Craig. He's a naturally gifted singer; never had lessons. I remember when he won our kindergarten class's Tiny Tots Talent Contest by singing the national anthem. All the mothers and the teacher got emotional when Craig, in his crew cut, shirt, and bow tie, stood in front of the class and sung like an angel in a church choir. My *Star Wars* Lego rocket ship didn't stand a chance.

The hairstyle's changed, flopping over his eyes while he's drumming, and the bow tie disappeared a long time ago.

Craig counts off, and the guys jam like pros. Right from the start, I'm in trouble. I'm strumming as if my fingers are dead weight. They eventually notice, and the music stops.

"Aw, come on!" Mick complains. "You should know it by now! We're gonna lose because of him."

"David," Craig asks, ignoring Mick. "You need a minute to warm up?"

"Yeah," I mumble and shake out my hands, embarrassed that I'm playing so bad. But there's no way I'm going to let Mick get under my skin.

The guys sit back and pretend not to listen while I quickly run though the song in my mind and on the guitar. Mick groans when I miss a note. I play it again to show I can do it.

"Okay, I'm ready," I lie.

We start from the top. Except for Mick, the guys are pretty patient considering this practice is important. We don't have time to fool around. For the past couple of months, the band has been practicing for QRAV radio's

Montreal Rocks Contest for teenaged bands. We just want to go as far as we can. Grand prize is the chance to cut a demo in the recording studio. It's something to shoot for.

Everything matters. Stage performance, vocals, rhythm, chords, timing, original songs... That's where I have bragging rights. While the guys can play instruments and write music better than me—for now anyway—when it comes to writing lyrics, they all suck.

It'll be the band's first public performance. If we win, it'll blow my parents away. But I don't want to tell them about it until we do, otherwise they'll think it's proof that music is okay as a hobby, but not a career choice.

I get through the song, telling myself that we're just warming up until Andrew gets here. It doesn't help that Mick's watching my every move.

"Hey, David," Todd says, when we're done. "That sounded okay, but you still missed a couple of notes."

"Yeah," Mick says, annoyed. "You're throwing us off."

"It's nothing practice won't solve," says Todd, who didn't entirely agree that I should join the band.

I'd like to throw Mick out of the garage. He's super serious about this contest and his music career. There are five guys in the band, but it's all about him. The others get fed up with his attitude, too, but Mick's the best keyboard player they know.

"How about we practice *Burning Rubber?*" says Craig. "David, you know that inside out."

"Yeah." I glare at Mick, just to remind him that I wrote it.

Craig counts off, and we run though the song with drums pounding and speakers blasting.

You caught my eye
When I was walking by
All shine and chrome
The sticker price I read

And my heart bled
'Cause I couldn't take you home

Then it happens. I miss a note.

Mick rolls his eyes.

I can't believe I messed up my own song! Craig keeps pounding the drums, insisting we finish. And we do, but I'm so bummed, I do it again!

Amazingly, none of the neighbors ever call the cops. Some of them are out there now, sitting on their front balconies, enjoying the free concert. Someone with a big head of curly hair–just like Craig's—is walking across the driveway. His mom stops to wave at us.

"Hello, boys," she calls out. "You sound great!" She gives us two thumbs up. "Craig, remember, show's over by eight." She points to her wristwatch, and then heads off to a neighbor's house.

Andrew shows up just when my fingers are warmed up and I'm playing halfway decent.

"Sounds good, guys," he says, slipping his guitar bag off his shoulder. He's being nice, but it's encouragement I need.

A streak of envy runs through me when he takes his electric guitar out of its case. It's a Gibson, like the one James Iha uses. It's a beauty, polished rosewood and maple; last year's Christmas gift from his parents. I'm suddenly conscious of my second-hand Yamaha, and rub at a scratch as if I can remove it with my fingertips.

"Hey, Andrew," Craig says. "Let's do it."

And they do, in spite of me. Some little kids on tricycles stop on the sidewalk and point. Andrew plays like an old pro, and Craig's voice is gold. I'm just doing the best I can.

The kids on the sidewalk applaud when it ends.

"Thank you, thank you," says Todd, and we all take a bow.

The kids pedal away without asking for an encore.

CHAPTER 3

QRAV's judges don't ask for encores either, but they know a good band when they hear one. These judges are awesome! The first judge, the man with the grey ponytail, is Kirk Lamarche, the producer who discovered Erik, a local rocker, and made him a star. The younger guy, Adrian Fabrini, writes a column for *The Gazette* on the local music scene. I respect his opinion, but some people like to challenge him, bombing his Facebook and Twitter pages with their own observations. And the third judge is Erik himself. His band's latest is playing all over the radio and is one of the top-ten downloaded songs this month.

The fifth band to play this morning is standing on stage under the spotlight, listening to the judges' comments on their performance. They played a tribute to KISS. They were amazing, and the judges, who are sitting in a roped-off area in the middle of the audience, thought so, too. They're going to be a tough act to follow.

This weekend's round is at a school in Pierrefonds. The auditorium is filled with band members, their family and friends, and a few headbangers in the front row. I woke up early this morning and got ready in fifteen minutes. My mother's jaw would've dropped if she saw how fast I can actually move in the morning, and on a Saturday, too. I packed a banana, a small bag of nuts and dried fruit, some Oreo cookies, and a small carton of chocolate milk in a bag for a snack. Breakfast was whatever I could eat on the way to Craig's: a butter roll and a half carton of orange juice. Craig's mom drove us. We had to get to the school by nine. I left the house before my parents got up, telling my grandmother, who was preparing rice porridge for breakfast, that I was going out with Craig. Luckily, we didn't have to bring his drums set; QRAV sets one up on the stage for band use, so we left as soon as I got to Craig's house.

The host of the contest, QRAV's weekday afternoon DJ, Theo the Greek, walks onto the stage. He doesn't look like anything I'd imagined. He's older, shorter, pudgier, and hairier.

"Let's hear it for The Arsonists!" Theo says into the microphone. The Arsonists exit the stage, soaking up the cheers and applause from the audience. "Okay, now give a hand to the next band up, Pumping Iron!"

I'm excited and nervous, not only because this is the first time I've ever played on stage, but it's also because we're going to play my song. The judges are going to hear it and talk about it. Talk about living the dream!

"Okay, guys," Andrew says. "This is it. We can do it."

After a quick round of high fives, we grab our instruments and head to the stage to set up. The audience is patient, but it's the longest five minutes of my life.

Andrew signals to the judges that we're ready. He quietly counts to three, and we break out into John Mellencamp's *Jack and Diane*. Craig's voice has that good old rock 'n' roll sound. That kid who had teachers and mothers cooing now has teenaged girls swooning. I'd have never believed it if I wasn't seeing it with my own eyes. The transition into *I Love Rock 'n' Roll* is seamless. The audience cheers and belts out the chorus, drowning us out. Then Andrew goes into his solo, guaranteed to convert anyone who doesn't already love rock 'n' roll. The audience roars, the headbangers thrash in time with the beat, and for a moment, I believe we can really do it. Not only can we win this competition, we can *make it*.

We're gonna be famous!

Drums, keyboard, and guitars are making music that defines harmony. We're awesome! I'm awesome!

Then comes my big moment. Andrew's guitar sings as he plays the opening chords to *Burning Rubber*. I'm rocking and really getting into the music. It's in every fiber of my being. But halfway through, as I turn to face Andrew, there's a tug around my right ankle. I'm still moving forward, but my feet aren't with me. Before I know it, I head-butt Andrew in the chest, hard enough for him to stagger back. I land smack on my hands and knees. Andrew, on his rear.

The audience lets out a gale-force-wind groan that fades and disappears into silence. Then the sound comes back like a boomerang, from a wave of giggles into a roar of laughter and applause, crashing into my eardrums; a deafening, embarrassing sound.

We had to practice our timing for months, but disaster always seems to get it right the first time. It's a spectacular ending to what was the beginning of a spectacular performance.

It was the day the music died.

* * *

"We're screwed," Mick says through his teeth, glaring at me.

"We don't know that," Craig says. "The audience loved us."

"We might still make it," Todd says hopefully. "We might get the sympathy vote."

"Well, I'm sorry we let him play," Mick mutters.

We line up on stage, waiting for the verdict. Andrew's

standing quietly at the other end of the line. He's not the kind of guy who blows up over anything, but if he did now, I'd understand. It would've been better if I'd fell off the stage and broke my neck.

When I landed at Andrew's feet, we stared at each other in shock, in the middle of a tunnel of white noise. The determined, pounding beat of the drums brought me back to where we were. Craig was staring at us wide-eyed, mouthing for us to get up. Mick and Todd played as if everything was normal. Andrew and I scrambled to our feet and started playing like mad, as the crowd cheered wildly. I don't remember finishing our set or even playing my song. It's all a blur. I was numb from embarrassment. *I can't believe I did that!* When we got to the end, I was shocked when the crowd gave us a standing ovation.

Theo gets the audience to quiet down, and there's a tense hush in the seconds that follow. Kirk Lamarche, the producer, begins. "There's no doubt that your band has talent. You played the classics in your own style, and that original song was very good."

The music critic agrees. "Your vocals are great," he says to Craig. "You could even consider a career as a solo artist."

"Loved your guitar solo," says Erik to Andrew, who pumps his arm in triumph after hearing high praise from his rock hero. He deserves it, too. The audience cheers in agreement. "You're a natural. As for the band's original song, it's not easy to write a hit, but, from what I heard, it's good."

I can barely believe my ears. They liked my song! Our song! Craig and I high five it.

"But that stage performance was a bit of a disaster," says the critic shaking his head, bringing me back down to Earth.

"Accidents happen," says Erik. "It's unfortunate, but you just have to get past it."

And then it's over. The news was good and bad. As we

walk off stage, I catch up to Andrew.

"Andrew, you okay? I'm…really sorry."

He doesn't say anything as he goes down the steps, but when he gets to the bottom, he stops and turns to me. I hold my breath. "Yeah, I'm okay, I guess," he says. "You?" His mouth is closed in a tight line, like he's holding something back.

"Yeah. I don't know how that happened," I mumble.

"Forget it," he says, saving me from begging for forgiveness. "Nothing we can do now. At least we got good reviews. We still have a chance to make it to the next round." As we head back to our seats, some people applaud us, telling us we sounded great. It helps relieve some of the pain.

We got good reviews with a giant "But" thanks to me. Now it all depends on how the remaining groups perform. We just have to sit and wait until the end to hear which bands are eliminated.

It's going to be a long day.

* * *

Theo the Greek is standing under the spotlight on stage, reading a piece of paper in his hand. I wish he'd hurry up and announce the bands that are going into the next round. It's been torturing me all day. It was hard to sit still and watch the remaining bands perform. Some were good, some were amazing, and some were just okay. Unfortunately, none of them had as memorable a stage moment as we did.

"Are you ready?" Theo growls into the mike. The audience settles down to hear the news, and I cross my fingers. "Let's begin. It's been a long day, so I won't keep you waiting any longer. The first band to make it to the next round is… Nails on a Chalkboard!"

A group of people sitting on the other side of the auditorium erupt into cheers.

"The second group is… Thorns of Destruction!"

We all lean forward in our seats. Todd's head is bent down, his hands balled into fists as if he's praying. Mick is sucking on the neck of his T-shirt. Craig's playing his knees like a set of tam-tams, and Andrew is taking slow, deep breaths.

"Unwilling Obsessions!"

"Blue Fire!"

Small groups of people cheer after Theo announces each name. A couple of them really deserve to move on, but I'm surprised by the last one. Maybe we can get the sympathy vote.

"Congratulations to all of you," Theo says. "And now, the last five bands to move on are…"

I stare at Theo, willing him to say the syllables that make up the band's name: *Pum-ping-i-ron*.

"The Sucking Truth!"

"Wizards in Flight!"

A pocket of people near the stage erupt into celebration. It occurs to me that if we don't win, I have a year to improve my guitar playing. Writing for the band and playing with them would be great.

Unless they kick me out.

"And the last band to move on is… The Arsonists! Let's hear it for the bands that are moving on to the next round!" Theo applauds, and the audience joins in. "To the bands that didn't make it, don't give up. You kids have a lot of talent. Keep playing, keep practicing, and come back next year."

Todd stops praying. Mick spits out his T-shirt. Craig's hands fall still, and Andrew stops breathing.

I swallow hard. "Hey, guys…" I start to say.

Unfortunately, Mick also has something to say.

"It's all your fault!" he yells, then lunges at me.

CHAPTER 4

I leap out of my seat and into the aisle, barely escaping Mick's grasp. Craig grabs Mick from behind and holds him back before he can do anything stupid. Todd gets between Mick and me.

"Boys! Boys!" says Craig's mom. "It's only a contest. You win some, you lose some."

"Yeah," I say, grabbing my guitar as Craig's mom urges me up the stairs, towards the exit. "We had our shot and the better bands won."

"We didn't get a fighting chance!" Mick snarls back, as the crowd sucks me and Craig's mom out of the auditorium. The air is thick with the smell of sweaty bodies and emotion. People fill the hallway, hugging the winners and consoling the losers. I push my way past them and stagger out the front doors. The afternoon sunshine is a relief from the glare of the spotlight.

I follow Craig's mom to the parking lot and slide into the back seat of her car with my guitar. Craig jumps into the front, and his mother turns on the ignition.

"Craig, I'm really sorry." I lean back on the headrest and stare up at the ceiling. The pain is going from the inside out, oozing through my pores. He fought to get me into the band, and this is how I pay him back.

"Forget it. The better bands won," he says, clicking in the seatbelt. "Don't kick yourself. It was our first performance. I didn't expect to win. We'll be better next year."

"It's not the end of the world," his mom adds, as we pull out of the parking lot. "You don't know it now, but something good may come of it."

"Like what?" I ask, confused. "I was completely humiliated! And we probably lost because of me!"

"You don't know yet," she says, mysteriously, "and you might never know."

Dr. Phil, she's not.

* * *

"*Olé!*" Bruno's standing in front of me, waving an imaginary cape. Some of the other kids in the hallway turn around and snicker.

"Very funny," I deadpan, pushing past him to my locker. "Come up with something more original, will you? I've seen that one a hundred times already." And I'm not kidding. It takes me less than a half-hour to walk to school and every step of the way, budding comedians let loose with jokes about using my head to play the guitar.

Saturday night after the contest I was still feeling pretty bummed out, and shut myself in my room. I was checking out Facebook when Craig sent me a message with a link and the comment, "You should see this."

I clicked on the link, and YouTube filled the screen. The picture on the video was the stage of the Montreal Rocks Contest. My mouth went dry and I broke out into a cold sweat. There were about seven hundred "Likes." The video was a minute-and-a-half long. I took a deep breath, and clicked "Play."

It's us. The guys. The band. The sound on the video is lousy. The angle is from high up in the audience. The picture zooms into the stage, capturing all five of us in a single long shot. There I am, really into the music, not paying attention to what I'm doing or where I'm standing. The wire connecting my guitar to the amp snakes across the stage beneath my feet. "Don't move!" I groaned, but it was way, way too late. I had been doing my rock star act, like I've done a thousand times in my head. Every cell in my body screamed in agony as I watched myself turn towards Andrew. The sensation of the wire around my feet was still fresh as I watched myself fall into infamy.

Real humiliation is spelled Y-O-U-T-U-B-E.

An hour later, the video has over a thousand "Likes." By the time I went to bed, it had doubled.

"You guys should change your name to The Singing Matadors," Bruno says, laughing at his own joke. "Then you can wear those cute little hats. It could be your shtick, like Blue Man Group or KISS."

"Get outta here." I dump my backpack into the locker and pull out books for French class. "Don't you have a class to flunk?"

"Hey, Todd," Bruno calls out as Todd heads our way. "I hear you guys gave a memorable performance Saturday!"

Todd shrugs off Bruno's taunt. "Hey, it's all part of the plan. No pain, no fame. Which video did you see?"

My senses go on alert. "What do you mean, 'which one'?"

"Oops," Todd says. "I guess you didn't see the dance version." Then he adds with a grin, "It's funny."

"I gotta see it!" Bruno cries out in glee. He turns and races down the hallway towards the computer room, a few other students at his heels.

"The *dance* version?" I moan. If Andrew didn't want to kill me before, he probably does now. "And did you have to say it so loud?"

"It'll be all over the school anyway," Todd shrugs. "Hey, there's no such thing as bad publicity."

"Yeah, right! That was my plan all along." The locker door slams shut, like the final beat of a drum. When I spot Craig approaching, for a moment I think that my best friend is coming to give me support. I'm wrong.

"Hey, dudes. Listen, I was thinking we should maybe postpone band practice till after exams."

"Sure," Todd says. "There's nothing for us to practice for now anyway."

It's not a shot at me, but his remark hits me where it hurts. "So when should we start up again?"

Craig and Todd look at each other.

"I don't know," Craig says, not looking at me. "We'll see."

"And there's vacation," Todd adds, uneasily. "My parents are planning…something."

"Yeah," Craig adds. "My mom's planning something, too."

I get the awful feeling that they already had some kind of discussion, and made a decision.

"So you'll let me know?" I look at Craig, who's busy checking his T-shirt for lint.

"For sure."

"I'm still in?"

"For sure."

Yeah. Sure.

* * *

It bugged me all day. Craig, my best friend, couldn't say it to my face.

You suck. You're outta here.

And if he did… I wouldn't have argued with him. Then in Math, Andrew avoided me like the plague. Instead of sitting beside me, like he has all year, he slumped down in a seat at the back, like he was hiding. Well, that's how it felt anyway. When some smart-ass no-talent kid cracked a joke about the videos, I shrugged it off, saying a lot of musicians fall on stage, even the big names. Those videos are on YouTube, too.

I know I screwed up, but I'm gonna practice and keep taking lessons. The guys can kick me out now, but when I'm really amazing at it, they'll beg me to come back.

So I get back to my routine: homework, study, practice guitar, and go to grad committee meetings.

Normally, I'd never join anything as lame as the grad committee, but last fall, when I found out Christine Ng was on the committee, I decided it would be good to show a little school spirit. Plus, I'm working up the courage to ask her to be my date to the prom. Everyone says it'll be the most memorable night of our lives.

It will be if Christine goes with me.

Our vice-principal, Miss Shirley, says the grad dance is going to be "good, clean fun."

Yippee.

"It'll be a grad to remember," says Miss Shirley with a sigh. She's got a far-away look in her eyes, as if she's reliving the good ol' days. The students have nicknamed her "Miss Shrilly" for the way she shrieks whenever she catches a student smoking.

The committee has been raising money for grad since school started in September. All the students in eleventh grade are helping out, and it's been a blast. Mr. O'Connor, our gym teacher, played bagpipes on a street corner to attract attention to our car wash. All the kids whistled when he showed up wearing a kilt and knee socks. And the bake sale in December was a hit. Pretty much everyone brought homemade cakes, cookies, and squares. The girls were impressed with my brownies, which I told them I made by myself, but came from a box. My favorite was the baklava that our physics teacher, Miss Voutselas, got her parents to donate. Then in January, we really raked it in the weekend we bagged groceries for tips. After adding it all up, we found we'd raised enough to book the ballroom at the Queen Elizabeth Hotel. The committee went to check it out a couple of months ago. The banquet manager, *Monsieur* Lalonde, was dressed just like I thought a manager in a fancy hotel would be, in a three-piece suit with a carnation pinned to his lapel. He gave us a tour of the ballrooms, or, as he prefers to call them, the "salons." Of course, I wanted to see the room where John Lennon stayed. Some of the other kids had never heard of John Lennon or The Beatles, but in the end *Monsieur* Lalonde said we couldn't because a guest had booked the suite.

Christine isn't in any of my classes, but we have the same lunch hour. She hangs out with her friends in their corner of the cafeteria. Lunch hour can be pretty crazy. I grab my sandwich from my locker and race down to the cafeteria to get a table. "Functional" is the only way to describe the cafeteria. You walk in. You eat. You leave.

Craig and I always sit with the rest of the guys, but if one of us isn't quick enough, we'll end up at the crappy table next to the kitchen door and the garbage cans. The best table is the one closest to the girls. That's the one I usually get. Close enough so they notice us, but far away enough so we don't look like stalkers.

I never noticed Christine much before this year. I always knew who she was, but I never *noticed* her until she and a few other kids ran a campaign to remove vending machines from the school. They got a lot of students and teachers to sign a petition. Most kids don't really care what happens in school, but if you mess with what they eat, man, look out. There was a huge outcry a couple of years ago when the cafeteria stopped serving French fries. Even the parents thought that was ridiculous. It was back on the menu within a week.

Bruno and I were heading to Math class when Christine practically jumped in front of us, holding a clipboard. She looked straight at me with her brown eyes, and smiled as if we shared a secret. Suddenly, I couldn't breathe and my heart pounded, like it did last Halloween when Craig, dressed in a zombie costume, almost scared the crap out of me when he crawled out from under my bed. Except this time, I didn't scream and leap away. I couldn't take my eyes off of Christine.

Her smile was just for me.

She finished saying something, and looked at us as if she expected an answer.

Luckily, Bruno was listening. "Hey," he said. "If I'm old enough to drive, then I'm old enough to decide what I want to eat." He held up a bag of barbecue chips.

"You can eat whatever you want," Christine assured him. She tilted her head back to look up at Bruno, who's the tallest player on the basketball team. Heck, he's gotta be the tallest seventeen-year-old ever. "All we're saying," she continued, "is that education shouldn't be limited to the classroom." She handed us a couple of pamphlets and the *Guide to Healthy Eating*. Her fingers brushed against mine as I took it. Was that an accident?

I hoped not.

"We should be learning how to take care of both our minds and our bodies." She looked from me to Bruno to the bag of chips. "Have you ever read the list of ingredients?"

"I trust my taste buds," Bruno said. He stuffed another chip into his mouth and talked as he chewed. "Besides, I gotta eat a lot if I'm playing basketball. I burn a lot of calories on the court."

"Instead of chips, you can have popcorn. It's crunchy, too, but healthier." She believed in what she was saying, so I did, too. Her dark brown eyes sparkled, and I had to fight the urge to touch her cheeks to see if they were as soft and smooth as they looked.

"You ever dream of playing in the Olympics?" she asked him, while shooting a glance at me.

Bruno shrugged. "Maybe. What about it?" He acted as if he never thought about it, but he had been obsessed with the basketball games during the last Olympics.

"Only the best make it onto the national team," she

said, in a serious tone. "You're one of the best players on the team now, but down the road, some other guy who's in better shape might take your spot." Then she looked at me, and gave me that smile again.

It was hypnotic.

"I bet your friends would like to see you play in the Olympics someday," she said to Bruno, while keeping her eyes on me.

Me.

Bruno looked at me, breaking the spell, and I nodded. Who's to say it couldn't happen? He took the pen from her and signed the petition.

So did I. And I wrote my phone number beside my name—in case she needed it—for the petition.

The grad committee meets in what's usually my history class, except Mr. James isn't there to put us to sleep. The room is just like all the other classes on this side of the school: quieter because it faces the football field and freezing in the winter.

School's *finally* over. It was a hard day. Everyone, and I mean everyone, saw the videos. Some kids were sympathetic. One guy even managed to put a positive twist on it, saying the worst was over and things can only get better. I hope so.

When I walk into the classroom, Christine and Elaine are deep in conversation.

"Hey, David!" Uh-oh! A knowing smile crosses Elaine's face. I'm counting on her reputation as a kind and compassionate person who fights for the underdog to *not say anything.*

"Hey, Elaine. Christine," I reply. "Counting down the days to prom?" So maybe I shouldn't count on Elaine's good reputation to save mine, but I can change the conversation.

"Yeah," Christine says. "Can't wait." Then she looks all concerned. "You having a tough day?"

Her question throws me for a loop. Nobody has asked

me that, not Craig, the guys, or any of the teachers who stopped the heckling in class. "Um, kind of," I reply, not looking at her.

"You know, you should be proud of yourself," Christine says. "It takes guts to get up on stage and be judged on everything you do."

"I guess so…" I'm not sure if I'm embarrassed because she saw the videos or by her compliment.

Then Bruno enters, sees me, and stumbles.

"That's not funny," Elaine protests.

"What kind of a friend are you?" Christine asks Bruno, who sheepishly tucks himself into a desk behind us.

Now I'm not the kind of guy who hides behind a girl when the going gets tough, but I kind of enjoyed that.

When Miss Shrilly and the rest of the committee arrive, we get down to business.

"We could have a theme," suggests Elaine, who volunteered to be in charge of making posters. She's an artist and is into expressing herself. Her artwork is as wacky as her clothes. Only Elaine would think of using a bowtie to wrap her thick, wavy hair into a ponytail. "Like the sixties. Then we can play all the music from that decade."

"Yeah!" I say. "Like The Beatles."

"The Mamas & the Papas," Elaine adds.

"The Dave Clark Five," Miss Shrilly says, with another sigh. Her glasses magnify her shiny blue eyes, so that they look like they're about to pop out of her head. "And I just loved Herman's Hermits." She looks like a lovesick teenager.

Christine looks at me, and we both try not to laugh. "Sounds like fun," she says. "Let's vote on it."

It's unanimous. Miss Shrilly gets to relive her grad.

"What're we gonna eat?" Bruno asks. Considering he eats ham and cheese sandwiches for lunch every day, I'm surprised he's concerned about the food.

"It's either pasta, chicken, or roast beef," says

Christine.

"We can choose as many as we want?" Bruno asks hopefully.

"Just one," Miss Shrilly replies firmly.

"The hotel sent me an estimate," says Christine, pulling an envelope from her bag. "And we should try to stay within our budget."

"Yeah," I say. "We should know how much we can spend before deciding anything." I glance at Christine. She smiles at me like we're co-conspirators. That secret Mona Lisa smile.

Cool.

"I know a really great band," Elaine says, excited. "They played at my cousin's wedding. We can probably get them for the end of June, but they won't be cheap."

Christine frowns. "Oh, I don't think we can afford one. Unless we plan another fundraiser, it'll have to be a DJ."

"Then it's a no-brainer," I say. "We get a DJ." Everyone agrees.

"All right then, so next week, we'll meet in the art room," Elaine says, wrapping up the meeting. "I got some of the students in art class to help make posters."

"I'll be there," Bruno says.

Christine looks at me. I catch my breath, afraid she caught me staring at her. "Are you coming next week?" she whispers.

"Wouldn't miss it," I reply. "Sounds like it'll be fun." And I mean it, too.

"It's going to be a great grad," says Miss Shrilly, as she slides papers into a folder.

I think so, too. Christine noticed me.

CHAPTER 5

These days, everyone at home is neat and tidy, afraid that the slightest misstep will cause a blow-up. Every morning the newspaper is picked up from the doorstep and placed on the hall table. Stray crumbs are quickly brushed off the kitchen counter, into the garbage can. Laundry goes straight into the hamper, not on the floor. But it's the mailman who causes trouble; a daily visitor who brings unwanted news. Store flyers go straight into recycling. It's those window envelopes from the bank and credit card companies that cause all the problems in this house.

This is the longest my mom has ever been upset with my dad. He feels really bad about it, too, and is doing whatever he can to get back on her good side, like bringing her favorite green tea ice cream home for dessert, doing dishes right after supper without being told, and washing all of the pans instead of leaving them to soak overnight. Most importantly, he doesn't channel surf while she's watching one of her favorite shows. Mom hasn't completely forgiven him, but at least they're starting to talk again, even if all she says is "yes" or "no". When she needs to ask him something, she sends Kim to give him a message. She asked me once, but I refused because I think they should act like adults and talk it out.

Neither of them will talk about how much money he lost. My mom forgets he never gambled before, especially when the bills come in. I sort of feel sorry for my dad. Ever since he lost his job with the clothing company, I think he's been kind of depressed. My dad would never admit it, but I can tell he's not himself. He quieter, and doesn't walk as tall as he used to. When he was looking for work, he looked a little lost, and wandered around the house or just sat in the living room and sighed as he watched Kim or me play video games. And he worried more, especially about Kim and me, about school, our friends, our future. It was annoying. We were relieved when he got the job at Kowloon Supermarket. It doesn't pay as much as his old job, but at least it gets him out of the house.

One evening after supper, I'm in my room practicing and dreaming.

And I'm jamming with Santana! The fans are screaming, "David! David!" For a moment, they sound like my mom.

"David! Kim! Come down!"

Oh, it is her.

I head downstairs. They're in the kitchen sitting around the table, surrounded by the lingering smell of cooking oil. Dad's drumming his fingers on the table, something he does when he's nervous or anxious. Not a good sign. Mom's at the other end, her arms crossed tight across her chest. Lying open on the kitchen table are a couple of those troublemakers: credit card bills. Kim runs past me and jumps onto a chair.

"Beat you!" she declares with a grin.

I have a bad feeling about this. When my dad lost his job last year, my hopes for a cell phone went down the drain and Kim didn't get a computer.

"David," Mom points at the guitar hanging from the strap around my neck. "You know the rules. And do you have to turn the volume up so loud?"

"I have to practice," I say, resting the guitar against the wall.

Mom leans her arms on the table and looks at Kim and me. "You've both been really good about not asking for new things since your dad lost his job," she says slowly, "but we're going to have to watch our budget more carefully now. We have to give up anything that's not a necessity."

The news is like a punch to the stomach. "Are you saying we can't pay our bills?" I'm numb, in shock. We're not rich, but we've never had financial problems before.

"We can't afford anything?" Kim asks, in a tiny voice. "Are we going to have to move?"

"No," my mom says softly. "We're not moving and we'll be okay, but we have to cut back on a few things." She pauses, looks at my dad, and then says, "You won't be able to sign up for dance lessons."

"No!" Kim cries out. She falls back against the chair and sticks out her lower lip.

"We'll see if you can go next year," Mom says, not looking Kim in the eye.

"But I love dancing," Kim pleads, on the verge of tears. She knows that if she bugs Mom enough, she'll get what she wants.

"I know." My mother cuts Kim off before she can go into full whining mode. "David has to give up something, too." She clears her throat and looks down at her hands. "He can't take guitar lessons."

It would've been less shocking if they'd told me I would be forced into an arranged marriage.

"Not the guitar lessons!" I shout. "I need them! It's my future!" Without lessons, I can forget about playing with the guys in the contest next year, maybe even forever.

"Playing guitar is fun," my dad says, staring at a spot on the table, "but it's not a career. You have to be realistic and concentrate on what matters."

"It matters to me!"

My dad taps a forefinger on the table to make his point. "You can't make a living playing the guitar."

"How would you know?" I demand. "You're cutting me off before I even get the chance to try."

"You can always take lessons later," Mom says, to calm me down. "And you can keep practicing on your own. Maybe your friends can help you."

"Don't encourage him," Dad says to Mom. "He's graduating high school. He should focus on CEGEP and university."

"Can we even afford it?" I ask, suddenly fearful that I might not be able to go. "How much did you lose?"

"Don't worry about that," my dad says.

"How can we afford university if we can't afford guitar lessons?"

"You'll go," he says, more firmly this time. "University is still a couple of years away. We just have to cut back on some things."

Another scary thought occurs to me. "What about the grad?"

"Well," says my mom slowly, "we already paid for the cap, gown, and photos."

"What about the dance? I already bought my ticket!"

They look at each other. Neither wants to answer.

"I need a tux! And I'll have to chip in if we get a limo."

"For the grad dance," Mom says slowly, not looking at me, "maybe it's not too late to get your money back. Or maybe you can sell your ticket to someone else."

I can't believe my ears. It takes me a moment to digest what she's saying. "That's not fair! You said I could go! I'm only going to graduate from high school once."

"Maybe he could," Dad mumbles. Mom looks at him in frustration, and he shrugs.

"Well, since you already bought the ticket... We'll see," she finally says.

"How could you do this to us?" I leap up from the

chair as if it's red hot and glare at my dad like an intruder. "You're always telling me and Kim that we have to work hard if we want to get anywhere in life. What were you thinking?"

He looks offended. "You think I did it on purpose?"

"What are you giving up?" I demand, looking at them both.

That's when I notice the grey roots in my mom's hair. They make her look old and tired. She used to color it dark brown, but I guess the budget cuts put an end to that.

My parents look at each other as if it's something they hadn't thought of. "We'll be working more," my mom finally replies. "I signed on for extra hours in the maternity ward. David, you'll have to help out more at home. Make sure your grandmother takes her medication and look after Kim."

From the way she says my name, I know I have to. The situation must be really serious.

I grab one of the credit card bills from the table and glance at the balance. The amount owed is huge. Is there anything of mine on this? I scan the statement. Of course there is. I never thought about how much it costs to pay for all our stuff.

Suddenly, I don't feel like an innocent bystander.

"What are you gonna do?" I say to my dad.

"I'm working extra hours at the store," he says, looking across the table at Mom for approval. She's busy looking at another bill. "Find a second job." He pauses for a moment, and then says, "If we all work together, we'll be okay." He doesn't sound as if he believes it.

I don't.

"Unless you blow it," I mutter.

His head jerks up and he looks angrily at me. "What about the hockey pool? You lost money last year. Don't fool yourself. That's gambling."

"That was only twenty dollars, not a lot," I point out. "I wouldn't do anything so stupid."

"You think so?" He says it like a dare. "We'll see."

CHAPTER 6

"Gentlemen, place your bets." Craig flips opens his chemistry notebook. It looks innocent enough. The edges are worn, the corner's bent, and doodles are scrawled all over the cover, but between the pages of lab notes and formulas is a chart of NHL stats.

Craig runs the hockey pool at school. Here at Trudeau High, there're rules about everything. We wear uniforms, blue polo shirts with a gold school crest, so teachers can tell who belongs and who doesn't. No cell phones are allowed in class, or they get confiscated and only our parents can get them back. The cafeteria menu has nutritional information on every item, but poutine with extra cheese is still the dish of choice. And Christine's campaign worked: the vending machines are history.

If he gets caught, he'll be suspended for sure. No gambling allowed at school, not even poker for dimes and nickels. A few of us guys crowd around Craig. It's morning break. Sounds of locker doors opening and slamming, and chatter fill the hallway. Some kid bumps me as he pushes his way down the jam-packed hall.

"Who's going to the Stanley Cup semi-finals?" Craig asks, in his best hockey announcer voice.

"Boston," says Mick, and hands him five bucks.

Craig takes the money and scribbles Mick's name on the chart. "Do me a favor, will you?" He reaches into his locker, pulls out a pack of cigarettes, and tosses it to Mick. "Go light one up."

"You know I don't smoke," Mick says.

"Neither do I," says Craig. "Come on. Just go."

Mick takes the pack and walks down the hall. He and I barely acknowledge each other these days. The Monday after the contest, besides having to deal with a few clowns, I had to listen to Mick mouth off to anyone who'd listen about how I screwed up. I got tired of hearing how I ruined his chance for stardom. Miss Shrilly broke up a shouting match between us after school, telling us we could cool off at home or in her office. Between his griping and the YouTube videos, I wasn't sure fame was for me.

"Okay, who's going to make it to the finals?" Craig asks. "Who'll get a date for the grad? Place your bets!"

Bruno waves a five in the air. "I'm going with Sid the Kid and the Penguins. And I've already got a date."

"Who? Your grandmother?" Todd asks with a snicker.

"Nah. She's going with Craig."

"That's cause I'm better-looking than you." Craig snatches the fiver from Bruno's hand, stuffs it into the back pocket of his jeans, and writes Bruno's name in the notebook.

"Who is it?" Andrew asks. "Francine? Sandra? Christine?"

My chest gets tight and I stop breathing at the mention of her name. The thought that one of the guys might be interested in Christine makes me ache.

"Nobody you losers know," says Bruno. He glances into the mirror hanging on the door in Craig's locker and checks out his hair. "She goes to another school. You'll have to wait until prom night to find out."

"You're hiding her? She must be ugly," says Todd. We

hoot and holler. He hands over his money to Craig. "Put me down for the Habs."

I let go a silent sigh of relief.

"Hey, at least I got a date." Bruno puffs out his chest. He's not the best-looking guy in the bunch, but he knows how to flatter a girl without laying it on too thick.

"So tell us how you do it, Romeo," Craig says, except I know that he really, really wants to know how. He doesn't have much luck when it comes to girls. Last year, he really had a thing for Sylvia, a girl in his English class. He thought she was *wicked*. When she dumped him after only a month, he took it really hard. Craig pounded the drums for hours after school, which is why his mom enforces the eight o'clock limit for band practice. Once, when I was at his house waiting for him to finish helping his mom with something, his computer was on, so I decided to check out my Facebook page. The screen lit up to a website on "How to Get a Date For The Prom." I only read a couple of paragraphs before he caught me. His face turned the color of a tomato. I was just as embarrassed. He swore me to secrecy, and we never mentioned it again.

Bruno considers Craig's question for a moment. "By being thoughtful," he replies.

"What? You remember their names?" Craig says jokingly.

"Make sure you wear comfortable shoes to the grad," Bruno advises Craig. "You're gonna be standing by yourself for a loooong time."

It's a slam dunk for Bruno. Craig's face turns red as the rest of us crack up.

"I don't know who to ask," he says, throwing his hands in the air. Then he looks at me. "Who're you asking?"

The question catches me by surprise. Craig may be my best friend, but there are times when a guy can't tell his best friend something, especially when it might possibly involve humiliation and rejection by the girl he has a crush on.

Especially in front of the entire gang.

The other guys are suddenly focused on me.

"Who're *you* asking?" I quickly reply.

"Come on. Tell us. Who're you asking?" Damn Craig. He can smell my reluctance. "Is it Francine? The two of you looked real cozy in Chem lab."

I'm getting really annoyed with Craig. "Hey, you're the one with the problem," I remind him, trying to sound cool even though my nerves are shaky. "But if you think I can give you better advice than Bruno, then I'm happy to help."

"Get outta here," Bruno says, insulted. "The only girl in your life is your mother."

"I have a sister, too," I say, trying to sound offended as the guys howl with laughter. Better that they think I'm pathetic than to find out I like Christine. They'd bug me about it every chance they got.

"Losers," Bruno says, shaking his head. "That's what you guys are. You'll never get a girlfriend."

"I just want a date for the grad," says Andrew.

"And if you want to get a date for the grad, you have to be thoughtful," Bruno says, looking directly at Craig. "For instance, I find something nice about her and mention it." He stops and looks around to see if anyone else is listening. We all lean forward as he lowers his voice to a whisper. "Sincerity is the key."

I know I'm not the only one to take a mental note.

"That's your big secret?" Andrew sounds disappointed.

"That, and don't eat raw onions," I say. Everybody breaks out in uncomfortable laughter.

Andrew looks a little hurt. "What if I like onions?"

We know he does.

"I'm kidding, man." I'm sorry I mentioned it. I could kick myself for embarrassing him again. "I like onions, too, but maybe don't eat too much."

"Hey, guys. Anybody for the Flyers?" Craig says, bringing us back to business.

I shake my head. "Nah. Lost too much money last year." I don't want him or the other guys to know that money's tight.

Craig smirks at me. "If you win, you'll have the money to take Christine to the grad."

A lucky guess. I feel my face getting warm and swear to get revenge on him, preferably something painfully embarrassing and in front of the entire school.

Suddenly, there's a high-pitched shriek from around the corner. All the kids in the hall are startled. Some head towards the scream to see what happened.

"Smoke alarm," says Craig. He shoves his notebook into the locker and slams the door shut. The other guys scatter and disappear in the opposite direction.

"Shame on you!" Miss Shrilly appears at the end of the hall, with Mick close behind. She's holding the pack of cigarettes Craig gave Mick, and is waving the incriminating evidence in his face. If Mick could stop smirking, he might look a bit guilty. "Get yourself down to my office! You know the rules! No smoking in school! You are in big trouble, young man."

"What?" Mick's mouth falls open in shock at the mention of the word "trouble". He looks at Miss Shrilly in disbelief and complete innocence. "I wasn't even smoking. I was just holding it!"

"A likely story! I caught you before you had a chance to light up." Miss Shrilly turns and continues down the hall, expecting Mick to follow. He does, but not before he shakes a fist at Craig.

Craig and I wave back.

I silently thank Miss Shrilly for the rescue.

CHAPTER 7

I'm walking up the street towards home and see my dad unloading groceries from the car. I forgot it was his day off. Before I can take a step back and think about heading to Craig's for a couple of hours, he spots me and waves.

When I was a kid, I used to go shopping with him while my mom stayed home with Kim. It was my job to keep track of the coupons as we walked up and down the aisles. He'd let me choose a snack to take to school, and I'd stand in the cookie aisle lost in all the varieties until he finally chose one for me. Sometimes, if we didn't buy ice cream or anything frozen, we'd head to Tim Horton's for a donut afterwards. I don't remember why I stopped going with him.

"How was school?" he asks, as I walk up the driveway. His tone is hopeful and his smile uncertain. Ever since that meeting about our family finances, he's been taking more of an interest than usual in whatever we're doing or trying to be helpful. Maybe he feels guilty that Kim and I can't take lessons anymore. Whatever it is, it's really irritating.

"Okay." I don't look at him, and pick up a couple of bags from the driveway. I figure if he doesn't have to explain his actions to me, then I don't have to tell him either.

I bring the groceries into the kitchen and lift the bags onto the counter.

"Ah, David home," Nai-nai cheerfully sings in Toishan. Then she opens the bags, pulling out the fruits and vegetables and inspecting them one by one.

Nai-nai and Mom are talking about what they'll make for supper this week. Now that Mom's working extra shifts, Nai-nai wants to help out more around the house, but since she's so frail, Mom only lets her do some of the cooking and dusting. And like Mom promised the night of the family meeting, Kim and I have extra chores.

"David, remember to put the wash in the dryer," Mom says, "and please, please clean your room."

"What's wrong with my room?" Mom likes things folded and put away, but I like things laid out so I can find them faster. It's a good system.

I cut through the living room towards the laundry room. Kim's sprawled on the sofa, watching cartoons. After my parents laid that bomb on us, she sulked around the house for a couple of days, but they didn't budge. At nine, she's too young to do anything about it, but not me. I have a plan.

"Hey, Kim, don't forget to empty the garbage. And you're supposed to empty them all at the same time."

She sits up and sticks her tongue out at me.

I leave my backpack on the stairs before heading to the laundry room. Opening the washing machine, the smell of stale, soapy water slaps my face like a fart. Pew-ee! I pull out a damp set of bed sheets with a pink cloud design. Looks like Mom washed another load. Funny, these don't look like they'll fit Kim's bed. As I'm shoving them into the dryer, some towels fall onto the floor. I pick them up and put them into the dryer before closing the door and turning it on.

"David," Mom calls from the living room, as I pick up

my backpack and head up to my room. "Did you wash my bed sheets?" My feet freeze mid-step. Is she talking about the white 600-thread-count, Egyptian cotton sheets that were seventy percent off that she swears help her get a good night's sleep?

"Uh, I'm not sure," I say carefully, remembering what I threw into the washer the day before. "Did you?" I'm running back to the laundry room before she finishes her sentence.

"Make sure you wash it with whites only."

And those towels that fell out of the washer were red.

* * *

A few minutes later, I'm in my room. Problem solved. It's why bleach was invented. The instructions said to pour a half-cap for a clean wash. Just to be sure, I filled it to the top. That should make the sheets whiter than white.

My room's smaller than Kim's, but it feels bigger because it's not filled with stuffed animals, crafts, games, and other kid stuff. All I need is my iPod, my guitar, and a little inspiration. The walls are a veritable Guitar Hero Hall of Fame. Posters of Joe Perry, James Iha, Carlos Santana, Richie Sambora, Jimi Hendrix, and The Beatles keep me focused. The desk that belonged to Uncle George is under the window. It's kind of beat up and the handles don't match, but it's my favorite place to sit and practice, or write lyrics.

Once, I caught my dad watching me from the doorway while I was working out the lyrics to a tune Craig wrote. When I looked up, he just chuckled and walked away. Well, what does he know about being creative? Mowing the lawn in neat lines is as creative as he gets.

There's no way I'm giving up guitar lessons. I'm not the one who messed up, so why should I suffer?

A notebook filled with chords and verses is on the desk, waiting for me to pick up where I left off. It's my homework for Mark. It'll be my last lesson this weekend, unless my plan works. I wrap the guitar strap behind my neck, check the strings, and then play a little blues melody to warm up. It's a simple tune, but it sounds good and makes me feel like I know how to play. I practice *House of the Rising Sun* until I can play it without missing a note.

My mind is busy with bars and chords; I lose all track of time. When I think I hear my mother calling, I look at the clock on the bedside table. The glowing numbers tell me I've been at it for almost two hours.

"David! *Hec fan*! Supper!" Her voice is loud and impatient.

"Okay!" The blank page I started out with is filled with scribbles. One part doesn't sound right. How's this, guys? My fingers scale the frets. The Hall of Famers listen closely, keeping their opinions to themselves.

"David!" My dad's voice booms up the stairs. "Come down, now!"

The Hall of Famers watch as I get ready to put my plan into action. *Hey, guys. Thanks for helping me figure things out. Wish me luck.*

When I get to the kitchen, everyone's already at the table. My dad stares as I walk in.

"You come down the first time your mother calls," he says with a frown, "and you know you're not supposed to bring that." I lean the guitar against the wall and sit at my usual place, across from Kim and Nai-nai.

Supper is boiled chicken with stir-fried vegetables, egg drop soup, and my grandmother's pan-fried dumplings. I pick up a dumpling and pop it into my mouth.

"Yucky! He used his fingers!" Kim scrunches up her face in total disgust.

My mom looks at me and sighs.

So I pick up my chopsticks, and dig into a bowl of rice. Except for the tinkle of chopsticks tapping the porcelain rice bowls, the five of us eat silently, conversation never being a high priority for this family. Right now, that works for me. I silently rehearse what I plan to say. A sip from my teacup, and I'm ready.

"Mom, I know you said we can't afford guitar lessons, but what if I get a job?"

"Doing what?" she asks. Scooping up a piece of chicken with the serving spoon, she drops it into my grandmother's bowl. Nai-nai acknowledges the gesture with a nod.

"I could work for Mark." Besides being my guitar instructor, Mark is also the owner of Le Grenier de la musique.

"You're not good enough to teach," says my dad.

"I didn't say I'd teach," I reply, fighting to keep my voice even. What does he know about music? Listening to the radio doesn't make him an expert. "I can do other things. Mark always has someone helping out at the desk, and I heard that one of the girls who works part-time quit."

I know what my dad's reply is going to be before he even says it.

"Playing guitar is not a real job." It's the same old song. He spoons vegetables into his bowl and continues, "You go to university. There's lots of interesting jobs that are steady and pay better than being a guitarist." He picks up his chopsticks and looks at Kim. "And you're going, too."

My sister nods. "Okay."

"It is too a real job! There are plenty of guitar players who make a living because they're good."

My dad shrugs. "It's hard to be a successful musician. You're too young to understand that."

"I do understand! I'm willing to work for what I want." I say this louder than I intend to. "Why are you always so negative about what I want to do?"

"David, your dad's right," says Mom. "There's more to being a musician than just playing the guitar."

"I'm being realistic." His calm, fatherly tone annoys me even more. "At your age, you can't tell the difference between dreams and reality."

"Is gambling to make money realistic?" I shoot back, and immediately realize I went too far.

The chopsticks sound like a crack of thunder as he slams them down on the wooden tabletop. We all jump in surprise at his outburst: a rare occurrence. My heart pounds from the shock of the noise and the angry glare in his eyes. Kim's mouth hangs open.

"*Ai-ya*," whispers Nai-nai.

"Enough!" Mom commands. She takes a deep breath before continuing. "It won't hurt to ask," she says to me, and gives my dad a look that says not to argue with her. And these days, he does whatever she says. "Working will be good for him."

"He'll never make it as a guitarist." Dad says it like he knows something I don't. "Music's a tough business. The guitar won't get you anywhere. You're wasting your time."

"David, ask Mark," Mom says. "If he says it's all right, see if you can work Saturday mornings. And make sure you keep up your grades."

"No problem!"

"Better you get a job that can lead to a steady career," says Dad, picking up his chopsticks and rice bowl.

"He can find another part-time job in the summer," Mom says.

"I'll be learning something I want to do," I say to my dad, relieved that Mom's on my side. "Nothing's going to stop me."

Right after supper, I make a beeline for the phone and call Mark, so my mom won't have time to change her mind. Nothing's going to stop me now.

CHAPTER 8

But there's a snag.

"Sorry, David," says Mark. "I wasn't going to hire anyone. Business is tough these days. When money's tight, people cut back on music lessons."

Don't I know it, but I don't say it. "Well, you won't have to pay me. I'll work in exchange for lessons."

He doesn't answer right away. "Well, I guess that's a possibility."

"It's what I really want." A gut feeling tells me he likes the idea. "Really. I was going to ask you about it."

"Heck, why not," he finally says, with a laugh. "If you really don't mind working for free, you can start this Saturday."

A smile grows on my mom's face when I tell her. "That's wonderful!" she exclaims, giving me a quick hug. "Are you sure you won't mind not getting paid?"

"I am getting paid, in a way," I say proudly.

Kim's mouth drops open. "You got it?" she says, surprised. "Mom, it's not fair! He's getting guitar lessons!"

Mom slings her purse over her shoulder and opens the front door. "David's working for it, but I'll tell you what," she says, with a smirk. "When you're old enough to get a job, you can pay for your own dance lessons."

"Not fair!" Kim pouts and stomps off to the living room, plopping herself down on the sofa beside Nai-nai for some sympathy.

Saturday morning, the alarm goes off earlier than usual. I don't want to be late my first day. After washing up and pulling a dab of gel through my hair, I spend a few minutes picking out what to wear, going through the closet, the drawers, and the floor to find something clean. Something I haven't outgrown and that didn't get mangled in the wash. Faded Gap jeans and American Eagle polo shirt. Perfect. I'm in the kitchen gulping down a bowl of cereal when my dad walks in. He's dressed for work, too, jeans and a short-sleeved button-up shirt.

"First day of work," he observes as he goes about making coffee. "Don't be late."

"I know," I say, stifling a groan. Everyone knows you have to get to work on time. D'oh! "I'll get there in plenty of time."

"Do whatever your boss tells you. You have a lot to learn on your first job."

"You think I can't do it?"

He looks at me and grins. "I saw the bed sheets."

With my guitar securely zipped into the gig bag, I strap it to my back and pedal through the neighborhood. The streets wind around aging townhouses and new condos. Suburbia on this side of the Saint Lawrence River means streets, parks, and schools that parents crave, and the boredom that teenagers loathe. On the other side of the Champlain Bridge is downtown Montreal. I live fifteen minutes away by car, but since my family rarely makes the trip across the bridge, I'd be as lost as a tourist from China.

The sun's warming up the cool morning air. It's a fifteen-minute ride to a street where most of the old houses that were built half a century ago are now boutiques and coffee shops. Le Grenier de la musique is in the biggest one. Mark and his wife Emily renovated the old clapboard house, built studios on all three floors and in the basement. I arrive right when he's unlocking the door.

"David. Good timing." Mark's older than my dad. He has more hair on his face than on his head and a beer gut, but he's a cool guy. He used to be a roadie, and toured all over North America and Europe. The wall in the waiting room is a tribute to rock 'n' roll. There's an old black-and-white picture of Eric Clapton back when he played with Cream, and a picture of the Guess Who signed by Randy Bachman. And there's the holy grail of all rock 'n' roll pictures, John, Paul, George, and Ringo when they played at the Montreal Forum in 1964. Now that's history.

I lock my bike to the stand, climb the concrete stairs two at a time, and follow him in.

Le Grenier de la musique is a really cool place. They give lessons for beginners, intermediate, and advanced musicians on all kinds of instruments: strings, drums, piano, and flute. My dad might think music is a waste of time, but one girl who took violin lessons here now plays for the Montreal Symphony Orchestra. Craig takes drum lessons; perfect for a guy who fidgets. The school sells new instruments, too, but there's also a bulletin board for people who are selling used stuff. That's how I found my guitar.

"It'll just take a few minutes to show you what to do," Mark says. "It's nothing difficult."

We go behind the counter, and I stash my guitar underneath. He opens the appointment book. The big black vinyl ledger is covered with a mess of names and phone numbers in pencil and blue ink. "Saturdays are pretty busy. People just show up for their lesson. Just check off their names. If someone calls to cancel, let the instructor know. We're full today, so if anyone wants to reschedule, put them down for next week." Then he teaches me how to answer the phone; what to say, how to put a call on hold.

Easy.

The cash register, with all those buttons, is more intimidating. He assures me that it's simple. "Just punch in the amount. It automatically calculates the taxes." We count out fifty dollars in coins and bills in the float.

"How many hours do I have to work to get a lesson?"

"Three hours should do it. You're working today, so your lesson next week is free. Do you want to have your lesson right after you finish working?"

"Sure. And my last regular lesson is today," I say, to remind him.

"Right," he says, nodding.

Emily, his wife, comes through the front door with a big smile. She teaches violin and piano. Her white hair is short, and she always wears a long skirt with a short sleeve or a long-sleeve T-shirt, depending on the weather. Her voice is as soft and kind as her smile, and when she does smile, her eyes twinkle. It always feels like she's about to offer homemade cookies and milk. That was before I heard her play the piano. At the year-end party last June, everybody's jaw dropped when she pounded the keyboard and rocked the house.

"Welcome to Le Grenier, David." Emily holds out a brown paper bag filled with fresh, warm poppy seed bagels and offers me one. "There should be orange juice in the fridge. Help yourself."

The door opens, and a mother and daughter enter. I check the ledger and tick off the daughter's name. The mother settles into one of the armchairs with a book while her daughter goes into the studio for a private lesson with Emily. That was easy. This job is going to be a breeze.

Pretty soon, it's busy with people coming and going. I get the hang of checking off their names in the book. I can do this blindfolded. The studios fill up as other instructors and their students arrive. I accidentally send one of Mark's new students to the wrong studio. D'oh!

One girl buying sheet music waits patiently as I try to

ring up the sale. When the cash register drawer doesn't open the first time, I punch in the amount again. Shoot, I think I charged her double! I start all over, and finally get it right. I have to remember to ask Mark how to fix my mistake. Maybe I should skip that blindfold.

The phone rings; someone wants to reschedule. I juggle the phone and the appointment book, flipping through the pages until I find her name. When everybody is finally where they're supposed to be, I get a glass of orange juice, lean back in the chair, and take a bite of the bagel. Warm, soft, and chewy, there's nothing like a Montreal poppy seed bagel. I eat slowly, savoring every bite, and look around the room.

It looks different from this side of the desk. It feels different. I've been coming to Le Grenier for lessons for awhile now. Forty-five minutes with Mark, and then I'm gone. But here, behind the desk, I see a lot more. Whether they want to be a star or just want to express themselves, everyone who comes here has a dream.

I'm polishing off the bagel when a man enters with his son, who looks about ten years old. "We're here for a piano lesson," says the dad, and tells me his name. He pulls out his Blackberry and looks at it.

I check the appointment book. "Your name's not here."

"Check the book again." The dad says it as if he's in charge and taps something on the Blackberry. His son's chin barely reaches the top of the counter as he peers at me through his wire-framed glasses.

I look at each line in the book carefully. "You're not listed. Do you want to schedule it for next week?"

The dad suddenly shoots me a hard look, which scares me. The deep wrinkles on his face are cut in stone. This is a guy who's used to giving orders. Someone important. Someone who never hears the word "no". I start to worry, and wonder what I said to upset him. Should I interrupt Mark's lesson and ask him to talk to this guy?

He leans over the counter, his eyes staring straight into mine. I'm leaning back in the chair as far as I can, but I can smell the peppermint mouthwash on his breath as he calmly whispers, "Listen, get my son in, and I'll make it worth your while." He reaches into his back pocket for his wallet and pulls out a twenty.

"I can't take that." He puts the money on the counter and slides it towards me.

"Just a little show of appreciation." He smiles like it hurts his face.

"Schedule's full." I hold my voice steady, so he won't know I'm intimidated. "Besides, the instructor knows who's coming today."

"Come on, help me," he says, friendly-like. The tingle up my spine doesn't think he's so friendly. "I was busy with work and forgot to sign him up. My son's going to be really disappointed. It'll be okay. Emily knows, I've done this before." He pats his son's blond head; he doesn't smile as he looks from his dad to me. "We're here now. Just squeeze us in."

Mark's words ring in my ear. *Schedule new appointments for next week.* "Sorry. You have to come back next week."

That friendly attitude disappears, and his eyes burn into mine. He sticks his forefinger into my face and says, "I'm going to complain. I'm a paying customer, and all you have to do is pencil us in. It's going to cost you your job!" Pushing his son ahead of him, they leave, banging the door behind them.

My heart pounds like crazy, and my nerves are jumping. The phone rings, and I leap away from it, afraid it's the dad calling to complain. After the phone blares a third time, I lunge at it.

"Le Grenier de la musique!" I yell into the receiver. Everyone in the waiting room turns to look at me. It's just some lady who wants information about piano lessons. I grab the brochure from the counter and read it out loud. She thanks me, and I hang up.

I don't want to be fired on my first day. What if that guy was an important customer? If Mark fires me, would he still give me lessons even if I could pay? I cringe a little thinking what my dad would say if I got fired.

When Mark comes to the desk to check on his next student, I'm both relieved and anxious.

"Mark, there was this guy," I say, pushing the words out as fast as I can. "He tried to give me twenty bucks to squeeze his son into the schedule for a lesson. I said no."

After listening to the whole story, his reply is a relief. "You did the right thing, David. Don't worry about him. You handled it well."

"What if he calls?" I eye the phone as if it's a bomb.

"Call me. I'll let him know I don't appreciate him threatening my employees." He pats my shoulder, and then calls his next student. They disappear down the hall towards the studio, leaving me alone with my fears.

CHAPTER 9

The rest of the morning is easy. Talking to students as they arrive and leave helps me forget that guy. And I check out the instruments Le Grenier sells. They have a basic acoustic guitar for beginners and electric acoustic guitars for intermediate players. There's also a couple of violins, a cello, flutes, and an upright piano.

Nancy arrives at noon for the afternoon shift. Her major is theatre, and she rehearses every chance she gets, like now, bursting through the door all out of breath, as if she'd been running for her life.

"Damn!" she exclaims, as she drags herself across the room. "I had to run six blocks because that moronic bus driver wouldn't stop!" She plunks the suitcase she calls a purse onto the counter, fishes through it, and pulls out a bottle of water. "David! You're working here? Cool!" Nancy gives the cap a quick twist and takes a gulp. "How many hours you working?"

"Just Saturday mornings." I grab my guitar from underneath the counter. "I've got my lesson now."

Nancy pulls her iPhone out of her pocket and drops into the chair as soon as I stand up. "Great. See you around." Her eyes are already glued to the screen.

Mark's already in the studio. It's a small, rectangular room and, of course, soundproof. He's in his chair, flipping through some sheet music.

"Hey, Mark."

"How was the rest of the morning?" he asks.

"Good." I take out my notebook and put it on one of the music stands. Then I slide the guitar from the gig bag, hook the strap around my neck, and sit in the chair across from him.

"Okay, David. Let's hear *House of the Rising Sun*. Have you been listening to the song?"

"Uh-huh. A lot." I play the chords he outlined in my notebook last week; a rock classic. Most of the songs I'm learning are from the sixties and seventies. I'd never heard them before I started taking guitar lessons. They're kind of cool. Mark thinks The Beatles' music is classic, just like Beethoven, and he's a big Springsteen fan. I've told him about The Black Keys.

"Good, very good," Mark says, when I finish. He's a great instructor. He makes me feel as if I'm making progress even when I'm making mistakes. Mistakes, he says, are an important part of learning, the school of hard knocks. "Now I'll show you how to bend notes." He picks up his guitar and shows me how to place my fingers. Mark plays a pattern, and it sounds fantastic.

I give it a shot. I swear I can feel the music, but it sounds like a cat screaming in agony.

We play the chord together a few times, until he's satisfied. Then he says, "Okay, David. Let's hear what you wrote."

Finally! I play my masterpiece, putting in all the feeling that the five-chord verse can hold. *My soon-to-be-climbing-the-Billboard-charts hit single...* After I finish writing the rest of it, that is.

He applauds. I stand up and take a bow.

"Not bad. Very good for a first try," he says, and then adds, "and very cool."

Yeah!

He writes down a new assignment in my notebook, *Hotel California*. "I think you'll like this one," he says, "and practice bending notes. When we get to the solos, you'll need to know how to do it. See you next week."

I bike home, flying high. I did it! At next year's Montreal Rocks Contest, we'll win, and my parents will be so proud and so sorry they doubted me. The band will be in the studio cutting a demo of my songs. My songs!

By the time I get home, I'm starving. A deep growl from my stomach forces me to abandon my bike in the front yard, in spite of constant warnings from my parents that it could get stolen and they won't buy me a new one if it does. I leave my guitar in the hallway and head straight for the kitchen, following a spicy smell I know and love: Shanghai noodles.

"Don't eat so fast," says my grandmother. She fills an eight-corner bowl with the thin noodles. I grab some with chopsticks and slurp them up. "You are so hungry," she says happily.

"It's good," I reply in Chinese, stuffing noodles into my mouth. She scrapes the pot, giving me every last bit, and then takes the pot to the sink.

The back door opens, and my dad comes in smelling of sweat and fresh-cut grass. Feeling his stare, I dig into my lunch. Sections of the Saturday paper are on the table. I pull out the sports section and try to read. Instead, I listen to the sounds of dishes clattering in the sink, cupboard doors opening and closing, and tap water being turned on and off, tracking his movements.

"So how was your first day?" He's behind me. I don't turn around.

"Okay." I clam up about that guy who threatened me.

"What did you do?"

"Answered the phone. Made sure people showed up." What did he think I was going to do? I already told him I'd work the desk.

He's standing beside me now, holding a glass of water. "When do you get your free lesson?"

"Next week." I take a mouthful of noodles, turn the page of the newspaper, and try to read an article about last night's hockey game. The sound of my grandmother washing dishes fills our silence. I hear him mutter something to her and am relieved he's given up asking me about my job.

Kim bounces into the kitchen. She climbs onto a chair, leans her elbows on the table, and sticks her smiling, curious face into mine. "How was work?"

"Good," I say.

Kim glances behind me at my grandmother, who is showing my dad something she wants from the grocery store. Then she leans in close and whispers, "If you got paid, would you buy me something?"

"What else do you want?" I whisper back. "You already have so much stuff."

She pouts and puts her fists under her chin. I think she's going to ask for another Barbie doll.

"Dance lessons," she says quietly, looking afraid that I'm going to laugh at her. "I want to dance." She sucks in her lips as if she's trying not to cry.

Laughing is the furthest thing from my mind.

"It'll be the first thing I do," I promise.

Glowing with happiness, she slides off the table and runs out of the kitchen.

Someone has to look out for her dreams.

CHAPTER 10

Every day when I get home from school, my mother is in a cooking frenzy. With one eye on the clock and the other on the stove, she juggles her determination to cook a balanced meal with being on time for work. The kitchen looks and sounds like a mad scientist's laboratory. Something is popping and sizzling in the wok on the stove. Scattered on the counter are open jars of strange dried things. A deadly looking butcher's knife lies on a bloodied chopping board.

Craig and I enter the kitchen looking for snacks to tide us over until supper. I grab the bag of chocolate chip cookies from the cupboard and orange juice from the fridge. The plan is to hit the books after supper and study for the Math exam next week. But that's later. Right now, we're going to play a video game.

"Not the whole bag," my mom says. "You'll ruin your supper."

"We're starving," I reply, and empty a row of cookies onto a plate, "and there's two of us." Then when I turn to put the bag back in the cupboard, she steals one.

"Mmm," Craig says, sniffing the air and rubbing his stomach. "Smells really good, Mrs. Chang."

My mom smiles proudly. Craig just got himself an extra helping.

We always have Chinese food. My grandmother won't eat anything else. I love my mother's cooking, but we eat a lot of the same things: stir-fry vegetables, steam rice, chicken or pork. When I say so, my mom asks what I want to eat. I answer, knowing what she's going to say.

"Pizza's not Chinese food." She won't order pizza. Ever. Except on my birthday.

"Why do you ask if you're just going to say 'no'?" Mothers can be so frustrating. Sometimes I get the feeling parents don't really know what they're doing. They make up rules as they go along. "When do I get to eat what I want?"

"Marry a Chinese girl," my grandmother says. She's sitting at the kitchen table, snapping snow peas. "She will cook for you."

"Marry someone who respects you," says my mother.

"Marry for sex," Craig says.

My mother raises her eyebrows, and Craig remembers the unwritten rule: don't let adults know that you know anything about sex. His parents are divorced. He assumes his father had an affair because his parents didn't do it. Craig's face goes red, and I get him out of the kitchen as quick as I can.

After we finish supper, my mother changes into her uniform, grabbing her lunch bag and purse. "Do your homework. Don't leave it until the last minute." Then she's out the door.

Craig helps me clear the table. My dad and Kim talk and joke as they load the dishwasher. My grandmother asks me to help with her medication. I'm in the bathroom squeezing drops into her eyes, when my sister passes by on her way to her room. Then I hear the front door open and close.

I glance into the living room. Craig's watching television.

My dad's gone out again. I can't believe it. Right after they gave us that lecture about cutting back expenses, he was home every night. Then he started being late for supper once or twice a week. Said he was working late at the store. So he says. I found a brochure for Gamblers Anonymous on the hallway table once. That was a positive sign, but these past couple of weeks he's out most nights and comes back around one or two in the morning. I don't think Gamblers Anonymous meetings last that long. What's he *doing*? He promised my mother, he promised us he'd change. I don't think my mother knows. She works the evening shift regularly now and doesn't get home until early in the morning, when he's safe in bed. I don't want to be the one to tell her, and I'm pretty sure my grandmother doesn't want to stir up any more trouble between them either.

It's Friday night, and the exam's on Wednesday. The text books stay in our backpacks and we play *Guitar Hero World Tour* instead.

The game is good old rock 'n' roll. Craig plays like he was born to pretend to be a rock star. His pimply face creases in agony as he falls to his knees and plays the color keys to a song about a girl who broke his heart.

"Think Miss Shrilly'll let us get a real band?" he asks, as he lies panting on the floor after his virtuoso virtual performance. Craig has decided that being on the grad committee might provide the extra attraction he needs to get a date.

"Not in the budget." I take the guitar from him and press the key for the next song. The music is flowing through my veins. My adrenaline is pumping, and I bend those notes in a way that would make Richie Sambora jealous. The animated crowd goes wild.

We play for another hour, until Craig develops a sudden craving for iced coffee. I offer him a Coke. When he refuses, I know it's because he wants to put his new driver's license to use. Nai-nai's on the phone. Kim's watching *High School Musical* for the hundredth time. It's just iced coffee. We won't be gone long.

Although the main street in our suburb has a couple of coffee shops, Craig steers the car across the Champlain Bridge and heads downtown. The downtown scene has everything a guy could ask for: pretty girls and pretty cars. The atmosphere is intoxicating, and we drink it all in like it's our first legal beer. The word "downtown" has a mystery to it, as if it holds the key to life. Everything happens downtown: the Canadiens hockey games, Alouettes football games, the jazz festival, comedy festival, film festival. When I was a little kid, my parents brought me to the Santa Claus parade. I gripped my dad's hand, terrified and excited by the crowd lining Sainte-Catherine Street waiting for the Man in Red to appear.

Craig's pumped with excitement, as if he's driving a Formula 1 car instead of his mother's ten-year-old Mazda sedan. Traffic is traffic, but on a weekend night, with the windows rolled down, the radio turned up, and the darkness of night covering our youth, rolling down streets lit with flashing neon signs is cool. Ice-cold coffee is the furthest thing from our minds as we crawl down Crescent Street, past nightclubs and restaurant terraces packed with customers and pitchers of beer.

We circle around and drive through the downtown area a second time, when Craig decides we have to check out the scene in Old Montreal, the historic section of the city that is a magnet for tourists and filmmakers. I'd prefer to go home, since we had left for what I thought would be a half-hour without telling my grandmother, but I figure he'll be bored soon enough and we'll be on our way.

Craig steers the car east on Sainte-Catherine Street, and we inch our way into the parade of traffic. It's slow, but we don't care. We drum the dashboard to the beat of street musicians and make fun of people with bad hair. When Craig whistles at a couple of girls on the sidewalk, I laugh more from embarrassment than amusement. Does he really think a couple of university girls would be interested in us?

We're not the only ones trying our luck. The sidewalk scene is filled with people on the prowl. Guys and girls check each other out as they pass by. There's a man leaning against a brick building, talking and laughing with a woman. They really look as if they're into each other. As traffic inches closer to the couple, the neon lights flashing above them reveal more about the scene than I care to know.

The shock hits my system like the headache you get with the first sip of iced coffee on a warm night. That man is my dad. The girl is young, probably in her twenties. She's wearing a lot of makeup, a tight T-shirt, and skinny jeans. A young Asian Jennifer Lopez. He looks happy, like he's enjoying her company too much.

"What're you doing?" Craig cries out, when I unbuckle my seatbelt and scramble to lean out the window to get a better look. Cars honk as we slow down and come to a stop.

"Dad!" I shout above the mix of music and motors from the surrounding cars. He doesn't hear me. The third time, he does.

Several people, along with my dad, look at me. Then he takes a couple of steps towards the street. Hands on his hips, he shoots me an angry look, which demands to know what I'm doing there.

I stare at the woman, demanding the same thing. He glances from me to her, and back to me.

We both know we're in trouble.

Craig grabs my belt and hauls me back inside the car. "What are you, nuts?"

"That was my dad," I gasp, and fall back into the seat, "but that wasn't my mom."

Craig turns down the next street and heads for the highway. We drive straight home.

CHAPTER 11

"Where were you?" My grandmother pronounces the Chinese words like we're in a tragic scene in one of her favorite Chinese operas. Worry lines crisscross her forehead, making her look even more fragile. Craig had dropped me off and headed home as I entered the house. Nai-nai stood in the space between the stairs and the living room, waiting for me. "No noise in your room. I look. You were not there."

"I'm sorry," I say, and give her a kiss on the cheek in apology. It's after ten, and she's usually in bed by now. She hugs me as if she needs to be sure that I'm all right. I wrap my arms around her, careful not to squeeze too tight. I'm afraid she'll snap in two.

"Where is your friend?" she asks, as she lets go.

"He went home." It feels like my head's going to explode. I was like a zombie on the way home. Craig talked non-stop, trying to make sense of what we saw. Maybe she was the daughter of a friend or a co-worker, but he didn't believe what he was saying either. When he suggested that maybe she worked at the club, it just made me feel worse. I don't know what kind of story my dad's going to whip up this time, but I'm not telling Nai-nai or

Mom. I don't want to be the one to deliver the news that breaks up the family, especially now that my parents are sort of talking to each other again. "Do you need to put in eye drops again?"

Nai-nai shakes her head. "Where did you go?"

"We went for a drive," I say, heading up the stairs to my room to avoid talking about it. I don't want to tell her what her son is doing. "He just got his driver's license."

"You are just like your father."

I whip around and look at her in surprise. "I am not!" I say, offended at being compared to him.

"When he was your age," she says, with a nod, "he always wanted to go out with his friends. Sometimes when I told him he had to stay home, he would sneak out without telling me."

"I didn't sneak out!" I say, with a twinge of guilt. So what if I slipped out this one and only time? That image of him and that girl talking and laughing is burned into my mind. I would never do what he does. Ever.

What's gotten into him?

The look in her eyes says she doesn't believe me. I swallow hard.

"Your father thought he could fool me," she says, waving a warning finger at me, "but I could always tell by the smell of his clothes."

"His clothes?"

She nods. "If he smelled like cigarettes, I knew he went to a *yeh jong wai.*"

She knew he went to a night club because he doesn't smoke. I don't mention that city regulations have changed since my dad was a teenager. Smoking isn't allowed in nightclubs anymore. It occurs to me that her hug might have been about more than concern. My grandmother's sneaky! I'm not sure whether to be upset or proud.

"What if they didn't smell of cigarettes?"

A smile cracks her concern. "Then he might have been telling the truth." She heads to her bedroom, sliding her embroidered satin slippers along the hardwood floor. It used to be a den before my parents converted it into a bedroom so that she wouldn't have to climb the stairs.

"Did he go out a lot?" I ask, leaning over the railing. "He told me he worked in the hand laundry every day after school."

Nai-nai stops and turns around. "He helped me wash clothes, and hung them on a clothesline before supper. Then he stayed up until midnight to do homework."

"So he was a good boy?"

She continues shuffling slowly down the hall. Without looking back, she flicks her hand in the air and sighs heavily. "He was a boy," she says, as if that answers anything.

* * *

The flashing lights are bothering me. Red. White. Red. White. And the faces under them are smiling. Him at her. Her at him. The only way to shut off the lights is to open my eyes and stare into the dark.

I'm lying in bed, wide awake, when my dad finally gets home. The glowing numbers tell the awful truth: it's three in the morning. His footsteps land softly on each step. The floor creaks as he turns left to my bedroom instead of right to his. The nightlight in the hall outlines his silhouette.

"David?"

The room's dark. I don't answer, pretending to be asleep.

"What were you doing downtown?" he whispers. "You left your grandmother and your sister alone. Something could've happened." His even, patient tone hits a nerve.

"If you're so worried, why don't you stay home?" I hiss. "You said you stopped gambling, so now you're out picking up girls?"

There's a moment of silence. "How could you think

that?" he asks, sounding offended. "I'd never do that to your mother."

"What am I supposed to think? You thought gambling was a good idea!"

"Your mother and I put that behind us."

"It's not behind us. We have to live with it every day!"

"Why are you upset? You're still taking lessons…"

"It's not just the lessons!"

"Well, it's not what it looks like." His voice is low and angry. "And I made a mistake. You make mistakes, too. At sixteen, you think you know everything?"

"I don't gamble like you!" I insist, shaking off a creeping feeling of anxiety.

"Not so loud!" he whispers harshly. "You'll wake up your sister."

I roll over, winding the bed sheet around my anger, and turn my back to his excuses. A soft light fills the space he blackened with his presence.

CHAPTER 12

Biology lab was my last class of the day, and my favorite. We had to team up to solve a crime, *CSI*-style, and examine crime scene evidence through the microscope to try and match hair and blood samples. It was a blast. Everybody had a theory, but in the end, Bruno and I solved it.

"The librarian did it with the candlestick in the kitchen," I said proudly, as we were proclaimed the winner.

"Yeah. It was a crime of passion," Bruno added.

I stash my books in my locker. The grad committee meets today, and Christine will be there. I take a quick look at my hair in the mirror hanging inside the door of my locker. Then Andrew walks up.

"Hey, David, can I ask you something?" he whispers. He looks uncomfortably up and down the hallway to make sure nobody's listening.

"Sure." He hasn't said much to me since the contest, so I'm surprised but glad he's here.

"Smell my breath?"

"Whaa-a-t?"

He looks embarrassed. "You know, tell me if it's okay."

I remember my comment about the onions. Suddenly, I feel the pain that I unintentionally inflicted on my friend. "Hey, I was just being stupid."

"No, man. You did me a favor."

"The girls like you, you know that." It's true, and that's because Andrew is such a gentleman. He always holds doors open and carries things for them, like my dad does for Mom. And like the rest of us, he uses colorful language when the guys are kidding around, but being the gentleman he is, he never swears in front of girls.

"Yeah, but you know... Dating..."

"Yeah." For a moment, we commiserate, sharing the uncertainty. Last year, Andrew had a big crush on a girl named Celine. He didn't tell anyone, but we all knew from the way he blushed and stammered whenever she was around. Somehow he managed to string together a sentence and ask her out. It lasted a couple of weeks before she dumped him without any explanation.

My first kiss was in grade nine. After explaining the Math homework to Sasha, she suddenly grabbed me and planted a wet one on my mouth. Then she ran off giggling, but avoided me for the rest of the week. Some of the guys make it a game, daring each other to ask out the hottest girl in class. Bruno doesn't sweat it, but I think he's just putting us on. I just don't believe that girls *never* say no to him.

"It'll just take a sec," says Andrew, bringing us back to his problem.

"Go ask one of the girls."

"Just smell my breath."

"Get away from me." I close the door to my locker and take a step back.

"Come on. Nobody else ever said anything. Just tell me the truth." He leans closer.

"Yeah, it's fine. You're okay."

"Don't brush me off. I need to know."

I've created a monster. "What do you want?"

"The truth." Then he tackles me with surprising strength for a guy who doesn't lift anything heavier than a guitar.

"Argh! Get off me!" I grimace as he huffs and puffs into my face before I can hold my breath. It smells... "Hmm, minty fresh."

He releases me and looks pleased. "Really?"

"Yeah. What'd you do?"

"Stopped eating onions." He grins and pulls a pack of breath-fresheners from his shirt pocket.

"It worked," I tell him. And I'm happy for him, and for anyone he talks to.

He salutes me with the pack of breath-fresheners and happily tucks them back into his pocket.

"So what're you gonna do now?" I ask.

"Gonna find a date for the grad."

I give him a thumbs up. He walks down the hall with a confidence I've never seen before. I silently pray he doesn't ask Christine. She just might go for a nice guy like him.

That's it. Time's up. I ask her today. It's driving me crazy, wondering if any of the other guys are going to ask Christine to the grad.

But I'll ask after the meeting.

So far, the committee picked a DJ, chose roast chicken with baby carrots and scalloped potatoes with chocolate cake for dessert, made posters, printed tickets, and checked out the ballroom.

"Ticket sales are good," Elaine reports, reading from her notes. "Looks like we'll sell out. For decorations, we have a banner and balloons for each table. I'm putting out a call for volunteers to help."

"Maybe we can have a green theme, too," suggests Christine.

"It'll look like Saint Patrick's Day," Craig says. "But if we do it, we should get green beer."

"I meant for the environment," Christine says to him.

"We could ask the hotel what they can do to reduce waste for the grad, like not using paper napkins and not using bottled water to reduce plastic."

"I think the hotel may already use cloth napkins and tap water," Miss Shrilly says, smiling kindly at Christine.

Christine's face falls, disappointed that her suggestion won't work.

"Maybe it's not about what the hotel does to protect the environment," I say slowly, forming the idea in my mind as I speak. "It should be about what we can do for the environment and for the future."

Miss Shrilly looks impressed. "Good point, David. And since we're playing music from the sixties, we could use the song *Big Yellow Taxi* as our anthem."

"By the Counting Crows!" Elaine says.

"Originally by Joni Mitchell," says Miss Shrilly.

"Well, either one would be perfect," says Elaine.

I sneak a peek at Christine. She's smiling at me like I'm her hero. I can feel my toes blushing.

I don't really care what the decorations look like, but Christine does. As she and Elaine start throwing out ideas, I support her suggestions with the right amount of enthusiasm. If centerpieces really can make a statement, then it's important to have them.

After the meeting wraps up, I linger, making small talk with the others just long enough so that I can leave at the same time as Christine. As I'm listening to Craig and Bruno talk about getting a bunch of friends together to rent a limo for prom night, I glance to see if she's leaving, and catch her sneaking a peek at me. She blushes and quickly looks away.

A flash of hope.

We all walk down the hall and out of the school. Miss Shrilly breaks away to the parking lot. Elaine and Bruno float off to the bus stop across the street. Craig says goodbye, unlocks his bike from the stand, and rolls down the street away from us. Then it's just Christine and me.

"So you really think including the environment as part of the theme is a good idea?" she asks. Her brown eyes sparkle with excitement and, for a moment, take my breath away.

"Sure. I mean, who wouldn't think the environment's important? Take a day like today," I say, groping for words and waving a hand out towards the sky, like a magician does when he creates an illusion. "A spring sky blossoming with clouds. This is where our future lies." Oh, God, please don't let her think I'm corny. That would kill any chance of her saying yes.

"True." She looks thoughtful. Like a lot of Chinese girls, Christine is petite. She barely reaches my shoulder, and whenever she looks up at me, it's always with a sweet smile.

"That was kind of poetic," she says, sounding impressed.

"Yeah," I say, with relief. "It kind of was. Well, you know… I write songs for Craig's band. Words, not music." I've never said that out loud to anyone before. It feels good. It feels real.

"Wow," Christine says softly. Her eyes open wide in admiration. "That's so cool."

I shrug as if it's nothing and stand up a little straighter.

As we walk past the football field, I calculate the distance to the end of the block with every sentence. I slow down a half-step to buy more time.

"How'd you do in history?" she asks. "I got a B+ on my paper about how the national railroad was built." She's proud of her mark and says it without bragging. That's one of the things I like about her.

My mind is busy trying to remember what those web sites said about how to ask a date to the prom, so it takes me a few seconds to realize what she's asked. "I did okay. I don't love history, and history doesn't love me. What program did you apply for?"

"Science first, business second," she says. "I think I

want to be a research scientist, like my dad. But then, I like the idea of having my own business someday. So I'm not sure. What about you?"

"My parents want me to study science, too," I reply, "or finance. What Chinese parent doesn't think medicine or accounting is the perfect career?"

Christine laughs. "I think a lot of parents hope their kid becomes a doctor or an accountant."

"Yeah," I say, "but I want to study music."

"Then you should do it."

I shrug. My dad's voice rings in my ears. *It's hard to be a successful musician.*

She touches my arm. "Do they know you want to study music?" Christine's concern and the feel of her hand make my brain cells scatter.

"Um, well, I got into the combined science and music program at Vanier College," I confess. "For now, we're all happy."

"That's great!"

"Yeah, but they expect me to come to my senses and drop music in university."

As we get closer to the end of the block, fear and words jam up my brain. How am I going to ask her? If she says no, then I have to act like it's not a big deal, and I'm not sure I can do that.

She's saying something about exams, and I nod and make noises as if I'm listening, like when my mom starts talking about relatives I've never met. My chest thumps harder. We're steps from going our separate ways, when the words burst out of my mouth.

"Bythewayyouwanttogotothegradwithme?"

She looks surprised, so I think I didn't ask the right way. Maybe I should've dropped down on one knee, or something dramatic like that.

But then, she says yes with a smile that makes my soul sing.

CHAPTER 13

We say good-bye, and I watch Christine cross the street. When she reaches the other side, she turns and waves, looking as happy as I feel. I wave back, watching as she follows the curve of the sidewalk and disappears behind a hedge.

Then it's like something explodes inside of me. Like when I hear an Eddie Van Halen solo. Every fiber of my being wants to jump and yell! I leap up and smack my palm against the bus stop sign. The metal sheet vibrates and a loud "Whaang" rings through the air.

Ouch. That hurt.

My palm is bright pink and stings from a scratch at the base of my thumb. Then I notice that a few steps away, sitting on the bench inside the bus shelter, is a little white-haired lady. Her face is wrinkled like used tissue paper. Her mouth is twisted, as if someone just told her a good joke, and she's trying not to laugh.

And she gives me a thumbs up.

Embarrassed, I manage a grin. I'm glad it wasn't my mother, or even worse, Kim.

But I can't stop grinning.

By the time I get home, I'm bursting with energy, so

when my mother asks me to pick up some vegetables from the Chinese supermarket, I run the entire way.

The Kowloon Supermarket is in a small strip mall on a boulevard not far from where we live. The automatic doors slide open, and I step into an atmosphere of Chinese pop music. The tempting aromas of roast pork and roast duck mixed with the smell of freshly baked buns nudge at my hunger pangs. It's no contest. I'll buy a pork bun and eat it on the way home.

The aisles are filled with food imported from Asia. They sell all kinds of rice: long grain, short grain, perfumed, and Japanese; and rice crackers in flavors like seaweed, soya, and sesame. There's an aisle devoted to instant noodles, even udon and pad thai. They come in all kinds of flavors: spicy, tom yum, beef, shrimp, BBQ, and seafood. I could eat a different one every day for three months. No, make that four. Then there are my favorite snacks: gingered plums, dried mango, shrimp chips, Pocky, green tea ice cream, and frozen dim sum or dumplings that we sometimes have for breakfast on weekends. Mom loves durian, that big, hard-shelled, spiky, ugly-looking fruit. It stinks when you cut it open, but tastes sweet. The store also sells household stuff like chopsticks, bowls, incense, and rice cookers. For Chinese New Year they sell lucky red envelopes for when you want to give money as a gift. When they put out stacks of fancy boxes of moon cakes for August Moon, it's a sign that the end of summer is coming. And once in a while my grandmother buys paper money to burn at the family altar, so Yeh-yeh has money to spend in the afterlife.

Lu Bin Fong, the manager, is in the main aisle, holding a clipboard and pen. He's geeky-looking and shaped like a football. "Hello, David. Looking for your *ba-ba*?" he asks. Although he immigrated to Canada from China when he was a kid, he still has a strong Chinese accent.

I wave at him, shake my head, and head straight for the bakery section, where I find freshly frosted butter rolls, plump and golden chicken buns, vegetable buns, and flaky egg tarts. They're hard to resist, and I'm drooling. There's less than a dozen pork buns left in the warming oven. I can finish the evidence before I get home. Mom'll never know. I pick up a pair of tongs hanging from a hook and put two pork buns into a paper bag. Then I head to the vegetable department on the other side of the store.

Two middle-aged women are pointing to cuts of barbecue pork and roast duck at the butcher's counter. Standing behind the counter are Kien Ly and Tom Wu, each wrapped in a stained white apron. Sammy Chin is unpacking boxes. He pauses to drum a catchy beat on them with his thick hands.

"Really cool, Sammy!" I call out. He beams and pounds at the boxes for a few more seconds, until Lu Bin yells at him to be careful not to damage the goods. In the vegetable section, I pick up a Chinese cabbage and a bag of bean sprouts.

"David," says Peng Chow. He's as short and round as the bok choy he's stacking into a neat display. "I hear you're graduating. You got a date for the grad?" He grins as my face grows warm.

"Yeah," I reply with a shrug, pretending to examine the bitter melon in the next bin.

"She must be pretty because you are blushing." He howls and joyfully describes my reaction in Chinese for the other employees. I slink towards the cash with their laughter ringing in my ears.

Tiffany Lau, the cashier, is a few years older than me, a little on the heavy side, and very pretty. Her eyes twinkle whenever she smiles, and she has a way of making me feel like I can't do anything wrong. "I bet the girls chase you," she says, as she rings up and bags my purchases.

"Nah." A few coins fall out of my pocket as I fumble for the money.

"David." The sound of his voice rubs my nerves the wrong way. My dad's standing a few feet away, wearing an apron and cotton gloves to protect his hands from the crates and boxes he handles every day. "You got enough?" He points at the change in my hands.

I wanted to get out without seeing him. He's looking at me, but I know he's only worried I'll tell Mom about that girl.

"Yeah." I say bye to Tiffany as I hand her the money, grab the bag, and walk out of the store.

The window is plastered with handmade Chinese signs announcing specials for that week. I pretend not to notice as he watches me through the uneven gaps as I head home. That was the longest conversation we've had since that night.

Anyway, it's not like my dad talks a lot, like my mom. She likes to hear about what happened at school or what we did at a friend's house. No detail is too small. And my dad rolls his eyes when Mom's on the phone gossiping with her friends.

My dad's more of a doer. When we were kids, he used to go bike-riding around the neighborhood with Kim and me. I helped him wash the car, and he showed me how to wax it without leaving streaks. We dug Nai-nai's vegetable garden on the sunny side of the backyard the summer she moved in. I had hoped that if we kept digging, maybe we'd get a pool, but that didn't happen. He didn't talk much, but he always did whatever had to be done. Whatever was necessary. Whatever was right.

I don't know what happened to him.

About half a block away from the house, I stop and finish the second pork bun, and then toss the paper bag into a neighbor's garbage can.

"Was your dad there?" my mom asks when I enter the kitchen. She's sitting at the table, helping Kim with her homework. Math probably, judging from the frustrated look on Kim's face.

"Yeah." The tone of my voice gives away my thoughts and feelings. I leave the grocery bag on the counter.

"He's trying, David." An apron is loosely tied over her T-shirt and jeans. Mom gets up from the table and empties the bag. Opening the package of bean sprouts, she dumps them into a colander and rinses them under the tap. "Adults make mistakes, too."

"So do kids, and you never let us forget," I say, fighting to keep my anger and disappointment under control.

The damp bean sprouts release a whoosh of steam as they hit the hot metal. The spatula scrapes and bangs the wok as she stirs, adding pork and vegetables to make chow mein. Tofu is sizzling in a small frying pan.

"You're working extra hours to make up for what he lost. Why doesn't he get another job?"

"He's doing what he can," she says quietly. "We have to be supportive."

"Yeah." I sit down at the table across from Kim.

Kim stares at me. She points to the corner of her mouth and says in a low voice, "You have sauce here."

I lift my hand to wipe my mouth. Kim grins triumphantly at my reaction. "Ha! I knew it!" she cries out and points an accusing finger at me. "You had a pork bun!"

"David!" Mom says, irritated. "You know you're not supposed to eat anything before supper."

"Why can't you mind your own business?" I mutter to Kim. I can't believe my kid sister tricked me. "And I only had one."

"I bet you had *two*," Kim says.

"You're such a pest." I flick at her homework, scattering the papers across the table.

"You're a liar," Kim retorts, sticking out her tongue. "And you shrank my purple sweater! You weren't supposed to put it in the dryer."

"I forgot! Maybe you shouldn't have put it in the basket with the other stuff for the washer."

Mom bangs the edge of the wok with the metal spatula. "Stop fighting," she warns.

"Don't worry, Mom. I'll eat supper. I'm still growing," I say, hoping it sounds reasonable. "Mmm-mmm, smells good," I add with a big smile.

"David," she says with a sigh. "Just set the table. Kim, finish your homework later. Clear off the table. Come on. Don't make me late for work."

Kim takes her time and slowly gathers the papers and pencils. I heave myself out of the chair and over to the cupboards. I take out five bowls.

"Just four," says Mom. "Your dad's working late."

"Again?" I ask in disbelief as I put one back. "How late does the store open?" If that's where he'll really be.

"They do cleaning at night. They can't do it with customers in the store," Mom replies. She opens a cupboard beside the stove, pulls out a couple of platters, and scoops the chow mein onto one.

"He never used to do that before," I say, wondering if that's the excuse he used the night I saw him outside the club, and if my mom believes him. "He's been working late a lot."

"That's all the store could offer in terms of extra hours," she replies. "Put this on the table." She pushes the steaming platter towards me, and then turns back to the stove and dishes tofu onto the other platter.

The plate is too hot to carry with my bare hands. I slip on a pair of oven mitts and carefully carry the chow mein to the table. If my mom ever finds out my dad went to a club with another woman, he would need an oven mitt big enough to cover his entire body.

"Kim!" my mom calls over her shoulder. "Tell your grandmother supper's ready!"

I pull off the mitts and hang them back on the hook. Then I open the top drawer and count out four pairs of chopsticks. The image of him talking to that girl, looking like he was having a good time, won't go away. I want to ask my mom if she knows what Dad's up to and where he's been. I've thought of telling her what I saw that night, but I know from the way she sucks in her lower lip that the anger is still there, even when she sounds calm. They talk now, but not like they did before all of this happened, when she laughed at his jokes.

Just before Craig's parents separated, they fought so much that he couldn't stand to be home. Some nights, he stayed over here just to get away.

I hope I don't ever have to ask him to return the favor.

CHAPTER 14

It's raining like Niagara Falls when I coast up to Le Grenier de la musique. My fingers are stiff with cold and water is dripping off the hood of my raincoat onto my face. The bike lock won't cooperate; I curse it until it finally snaps shut. There's no point in sprinting to the door to get out of the rain since I'm already wet, but I do it anyway.

I shake off my raincoat and hang it in the closet. My jeans are stiff with water below the knees. I try to wring out whatever I can. I open the case to check my guitar, relieved it's dry. The smell of fresh coffee drifts in from the kitchen. Emily's talking to a couple of instructors. She turns around, smiles, and waves at me.

All morning, people arrive with dripping umbrellas and wet shoes. They stamp their feet but still leave puddles of footprints on the floor. Now I'll have to mop up after everyone.

I'm checking off names as people arrive, when Craig comes up to the desk. I put a tick beside his name in the appointment book.

"Hey, David. What're you doing after work?

"Got a lesson. Why?"

"Some of the guys are going to the movies. Wanna go?"

I don't have any money, but Craig doesn't know that I don't get paid. I can't ask my parents for any after I made such a stink about working for free. "I don't know," I say, glancing down at the desk, looking for an excuse.

"Okay. If you wanna come, meet us at the theatre. Movie starts at two." Then he heads off for his drumming lesson.

I want to go. I deserve it. I haven't asked for anything since this whole mess started.

After all the studio doors close, I pick up the phone and call home. My mom's not there, so I ask my grandmother to tell her to call me at work. When Craig comes out a half-hour later, he signals for me to call him, then yanks a hood over his head and disappears out the door, into the storm.

When my mom phones, she sighs. "David, I just told Kim we couldn't go to a movie."

"So let her go, too," I say, knowing in my gut where this conversation is heading. "That's fair." A couple of mothers are sitting next to the window, waiting for their kids. They glance at me and grin at each other. I'm embarrassed they heard me begging for permission.

There's another sigh, and then a pause. "No, David."

"Just this once," I whisper into the phone.

"David, you know we can't."

"Yeah, I know." I hate that I do. I bet she wouldn't be so tough on me if she knew my dad was still sneaking out at night. I hang up.

A mother is urging her twin daughters into their raincoats. Their violin cases lie open on the floor. I go over to help pack up their instruments as the mother tries to get the restless seven-year-olds to cooperate.

"Thanks," she says, looking grateful. "By the way, I need sheet music." She hands me a piece of paper.

I snap the last case shut, go over to the rack display,

and find what she needs. When I hand it to her, she gives me some bills. "Here, this should cover it." She tucks the sheet music into her bag, grabs her daughters' hands, and heads out the door.

"Wait, your change," I call after her.

"Keep it. It's only a nickel." Then they're gone.

A kid taps my arm. "Can you help us?" He points to his dad, who's looking at the guitars on display. "Which one should I get?"

I spend a few minutes showing them guitars and giving a little demonstration. The kid is impressed, and the father doesn't have a clue. A shriek interrupts my performance. A lady slipped and almost fell in the hall, so I grab the mop from the closet and clean up the floor. For the last hour, I answer questions on courses, phone students to cancel next week's cello lessons, and mop the floor again and again.

By the time my lesson's over, the rain has stopped. I bike home, a feeling of frustration in my gut. If I can't even afford to go to a movie, how am I going to take Christine to the grad? Maybe if I skip a couple of lessons, I can ask Mark to pay me. But I don't really want to ask him, since he only hired me because I said I'd work for free.

The sky turns blue as white clouds push away the dark ones. My raincoat feels hot and sticky against my skin. I pedal faster down the street, but not even the breeze cools me off. I coast up our driveway and stick my hand into my back pocket for the key. Instead, I come up with a fistful of money.

The mother with the twins.

I forgot to ring up the sale.

My first instinct is to bike all the way back to the store. But they wouldn't miss the money today, would they? I stare at the crumpled bills in my hand, more than enough to go to the movies and get some popcorn.

I can give the money back next Saturday.

So what if I forgot to put the money in the cash

register? If I put it back next Saturday, then there's no harm in using it now. Nobody saw me put the money in my pocket. The mother rushed out right after she handed it to me.

I'll just borrow it. It's not like I mean to steal it.

My grandmother and Kim are in the living room watching television. I race up the stairs two at a time and put the guitar in my room.

"Where are you going?" My grandmother looks at me when I reach the bottom of the stairs.

There's a knot in my chest, and I stammer as if I've been caught red-handed. I swallow hard. "I'm going out with Craig." I glance at my watch. Thirty minutes until the movie starts.

I run out, hop on my bike, and pedal like I'm on the lam.

CHAPTER 15

All the plans for the dance are finished. The grad committee doesn't meet anymore, but I still walk Christine part of the way home. I meet her after school. It helps that I memorized her schedule. I got a peek at the binder she left open on a desk at the last meeting.

The bell rings, and I'm the first one out of Math class. I race down the hallway that stretches from one end of the school to the other, zigging and zagging around the students pouring out of their classrooms. As I skid around the corner, I see Christine coming down the hallway with a couple of friends. I hang back to catch my breath. They see me, and Christine breaks into a smile.

"Going home?" I ask, trying to sound cool and not like an old man wheezing for breath.

Her eyes sparkle, and she nods.

The students stampede towards the exits, swallowing up her friends. The chatter and thunderous footsteps in the hallway and leading out through the doors is loud, but the only person I can hear is Christine.

"I was hoping to see you," she says shyly.

And everything feels all right. Our fingers brush as we walk side by side, and she blushes.

When we reach the sidewalk, someone calls my name. It's Craig. He runs over and spits out the news.

"A band? A live band?" Christine repeats in disbelief.

"I thought there wasn't any money," I say.

Craig nods. "There isn't. Shrilly said so. They're playing for free."

"How come she told you?" I ask Craig.

"She didn't," he says with a grin. "I heard her tell Miss Voutselas about it."

The news that a live band is going to play at the grad spreads around the school faster than a pirated song. There's a lot of excitement, like it's a big deal. Like we're a big deal. When we find out the name of the band is a secret, the rumors run wild.

A famous band is using our grad to make a video.

A famous band is using our grad to record their next hit.

The ultimate rumor, and my favorite, is the band is part of a reality show.

Since we're on the grad committee, Bruno, Elaine, Christine, Craig, and I figure we have the right to know. We storm Miss Shrilly's office asking questions and demanding answers. But no matter what we say, Miss Shrilly brings her hand to her mouth, twists her wrist like she's locking her lips, and throws away the imaginary key.

And she looks pleased with herself, too.

After a couple of days with nothing new to report, the news about the band dies down. Nothing to do but hit the books. Craig and I temporarily put away our dreams of being rock stars and hang out at the library during free period. I go hoping to see Christine. Craig's still looking for a date.

When the bell rings, signaling the end of first period, I join the stream of students heading down the stairwell. The library is on the first floor, at the end of a peeling and cracked corridor. Class pictures of students who graduated before I was born hang on the walls like an honor roll. As

I pass by Administration, I glance through the glass pane in the door. A man stands at the beat-up wooden counter, talking to Miss Shrilly. His back is to me, but I recognize the profile, clothes, and haircut. She looks up into my startled face, and smiles.

Then my dad turns around.

He looks as surprised to see me as I am to see him, which is weird because I'm supposed to be here. The first thing that pops into my head is that I'm in trouble. But I didn't do anything wrong, so that can't be it. There are papers on the counter that seem to be the center of their attention.

Miss Shrilly sweeps them up and holds them close to her chest. "What a coincidence that you drop by when your dad's here." The papers disappear into a folder and under the counter.

He thanks her, says he'll be in touch, and leaves the office. I follow him.

"What are you doing here?" I whisper. The hallway is almost deserted as students disappear into classrooms.

"Shouldn't you be in class?"

"Yeah," I reply, irritated that he's avoiding the question. "So what?"

"You should get going."

"What are you *doing* here?" I press him again, my suspicions growing by the second.

My dad sighs. "Well, it's your last year, and I had some business with the school."

"What business? Nobody else's parents had to come. Why you?"

"Don't worry about it," he says, pretending to be absorbed in the old pictures on the wall.

"Don't worry? You were in the principal's office. What am I supposed to think?"

"Did you do something you want to tell me about?" he jokes. Then he waves good-bye, and quickly walks out the door.

I don't feel like joking. My mom has always been the one who signs report cards and permission slips for field trips, and attends parent-teacher meetings. Seeing my dad here was weird.

As soon as I get home, I tell my mom about it, but she shrugs it off. If I didn't know any better, I'd say they were in cahoots.

"Don't worry about it. You're not in any trouble," she says, heading towards the laundry room.

I point at the basket she's carrying, overflowing with laundry. "Shouldn't I be doing that?"

She looks at me with a grimace. "It'll cost us less if I do it. You can do the vacuuming from now on."

CHAPTER 16

My life is crap.

Bad enough we're in the hole financially. My dad's having an affair with a girl half his age, I can't find out what my dad was doing in the principal's office 'cause Miss Shrilly won't talk, and I don't know where I'm going to find twenty bucks. Then today at work, Craig reminds me to get a tux.

And how am I supposed to pay for that?

Crap.

The thing to do now is eat. I think better on a full stomach. The pork-fried rice warming in the wok has my full attention. I stir it a little to make sure it's heated through, and then grab a dish from the cupboard.

Just as I'm sitting down at the table, my grandmother shuffles into the kitchen. She grunts as she lowers herself into a chair. One of her favorite pastimes is watching me eat. She's happy that I have such a healthy appetite.

"Ah, David," she says, "did you get good marks?"

"Not yet," I reply in Chinese. "I still have exams."

"Wong *Tai* said her grandson is going to be a doctor. Do you want to be a doctor?"

I make a face, and she laughs.

"You will go to university?" she asks.

My mouth is busy appreciating lunch, so I nod.

A big smile breaks out on her face. "You are a good boy," she says. "You go to school and be a professional."

The adults in my family are way too obsessed with the word "professional." When they say *that* word, they mean an accountant, a lawyer, or a doctor. A businessman. Nai-nai looks so happy that I don't have the heart to tell her I really want to be a musician.

Well, a *professional* musician.

Kim skips into the kitchen and climbs onto the chair beside me. My mom is close behind and stands next to Nai-nai.

"Ma," my mom says to my grandmother. "Did you tell him?"

My grandmother shakes her head.

"What?" I ask, suspicious of the cheerful faces before me.

"David," my mom says, "we have a surprise graduation present for you." She and my grandmother look at each other. "We're going to find you a suit for grad. You'll look good for your date."

I can't believe my ears. This is a miracle. "I can go?" I ask, saying it slowly to make sure they understand what I'm saying.

Mom looks down at her feet for a second. "Nai-nai wants to buy it for you," she says softly. My parents are embarrassed that Nai-nai has been helping out with more of the bills. Nai-nai gave Dad some cash the other day for groceries. He didn't want to take it, but she insisted. I was a little worried about him having all that money, but was relieved when I saw him hauling bags of food out of the car a couple of hours later.

"How did you know I have a date?" I ask.

Kim, who is making a mess on the table cracking open lychee nuts, smirks at me. The tattletale discovered my secret. It's the first time it's worked in my favor.

"You're so nosy," I complain to Kim, relieved I don't have to beg for a suit. "How'd you find out?"

"Bruno's sister is in my class," Kim says, pleased with herself. She crosses her arms and sits back in the chair, enjoying the moment. "I was playing at her house when Bruno told their parents he was going to rent a limousine."

"Yeah, so? Anybody can rent a limousine." It's a weak point, but I can't think of anything else.

"He was counting the number of people going. He was counting two by two, just like Noah's Ark."

Damn, she's smart. "You should be a gossip columnist when you grow up," I say.

Kim grins. "Maybe I will be."

"It won't be anything fancy," Mom warns. "We'll check out the sales and the outlets." Then she looks at me with a big smile. "Who are you going with?"

I look at Kim and feign shock. "What? You didn't figure that out? Guess you're not that good."

"I would have if I'd had more time," Kim says defensively. "So? Who's the unlucky girl?"

I concentrate on picking up the last grains of rice with my chopsticks. "Christine Ng." My face is getting warm, and I don't want them to see me blush.

"Is her father a research scientist?" Mom asks. Of course, she would know of him. He probably works at the hospital.

"Yeah."

"Oooo-oh." From the musical tone in Mom's voice, I can tell she's pleased. "Well, we'll go as soon as you're finished eating. Nai-nai wants to visit Lau *Tai*, so we'll drop her off on our way."

"I want a black suit," I tell my mom.

"You'll be able to wear it to weddings and funerals," Kim says knowingly.

"So now you're a fashion consultant?" I say.

"Lucky for you," she says, "or you'll look like a dork."

"Thank you, Nai-nai," I say in Chinese. "It's exactly

what I want."

She smiles and laughs as if I couldn't have said anything else that would have made her happier.

* * *

The outlets are only a half-hour away. After we drop Nai-nai off at Mrs. Lau's house, we take the highway and head east. Cars line up to get into the gigantic parking lot. We drive up and down rows of cars until we find a spot between an SUV and a minivan.

One of the biggest stores is a popular discount store. Shoppers dig through racks of clothing like they're searching for buried treasure. Shopping is not on my list of top-ten ways to spend a Saturday. Not like girls, who spend all their time at the mall looking at things they'll never buy. I know what I like. I'm in and out of a store in minutes. T-shirts and jeans are easy. Find my size, and I'm done.

But finding a suit is a lot harder.

Mom checks out the liquidation rack first and hits pay dirt: a black two-piece and a dark grey three-piece suit. It takes longer to find a shirt and tie. We can't agree on whether I should wear a white shirt or a dark color. I head for the changing room with both.

My mom doesn't like how the black suit fits. Neither do I. And the grey suit doesn't look right for a prom. I hand the pile of clothes to the sales girl, and we go back to the racks.

The three of us can't agree on anything. If I like the style, then my mom doesn't like the price tag. If the price is okay, then either Kim or I don't like the style or color.

"Don't be so picky," my mom says, frustrated, as we head out to another store.

A couple of stores later, I'm as edgy as my mom. This one has suits and prom dresses in the window. Girls giggle as they carry armfuls of dresses to the fitting room.

"Do you want a nice suit for your prom or not?" Mom hisses. The one she's holding is worse than the one before. Kim rolls her eyes.

"The pockets don't look good," I say, "and the collar's too wide."

"It's retro," Mom says. "The seventies are back in style. Try it on."

"No," I reply. "It's been there for years. Nobody buys it because it's ugly."

Exasperated, Mom shoves the suit back on the rack.

"Can I help you?" asks a salesman. He's been keeping an eye on us, sniffing out a potential sale.

"No, thanks," I say, disappointed.

"Have you thought about renting a tux?" the salesman asks.

My mom and I look at each other. "Isn't it more expensive?" she asks.

"No," the salesman says. "It depends on how much you want to spend. And the suit you buy today might not fit him next year."

Mom groans.

"Do you have any?" I ask.

He shakes his head. "But we do at our other store. I can give you the address."

We follow him to the counter.

Thirty minutes later, I stand in front of a three-way mirror, admiring myself in a black three-piece tux. As the salesman fusses with the sleeves and pant legs, he explains to my mom that the tux will have to be ordered, and it comes complete with a white shirt, vest, bow tie, socks, and shoes. I get to keep the socks.

"Ohh!" Kim says in surprise. "You look *good*."

Mom agrees, looking as relieved as I feel.

Christine will find me irresistible.

"Find out what Christine's wearing," Mom says to me, as the salesman writes up the order. "If she's wearing a strapless dress, you'll have to get a wrist corsage." I look at her in disbelief. "Don't worry, I'll pay for it," she adds.

"Who are you, and what have you done with my mother?" I say, faking horror. Mom twists her mouth, trying not to laugh, and hands the salesman a credit card.

On our way home, we go to Mrs. Lau's house and pick up Nai-nai. At supper, Mom shows me how I should help Christine sit at the table. "Just push the chair in a little, not too far and not too fast," Mom says, as I slide the chair under her.

After the dishes are packed into the dishwasher, she offers to show me how to dance. The last dance I went to was my elementary school graduation party. All the boys stood on one side of the gym and the girls on the other. There was very little dancing. I take her up on the offer.

I mean, it's not like anyone's going to see.

It's one of her rare nights off. She's giddy and ready to have fun. The velvety voice of Michael Bublé fills the living room. I make sure the curtains are closed tight. You never know who might be walking by. Nai-nai sits on the sofa to watch.

We dance. My mom sways to the music, snapping her fingers, twisting and bouncing to the rhythm. I've never seen her dance before, and I'm surprised at how good she is. Kim leaps around the living room as if she's auditioning for *So You Think You Can Dance*.

"Guys don't dance like that," I say to my mom. Then, before Kim can open her mouth, I add. "Regular guys, I mean."

"Maybe we should start off with the basics," Mom says, and presses the forward button on the stereo to a slower song. Soft piano notes float out of the speakers. I think I can handle this.

"You put your arms like this." She adjusts my arms so that one hand is in hers and the other on her shoulder. "Then you step forward, and I step backward."

I step right on her toes.

"Ow! Together! Together," she winces. "Kim, you

count."

Kim counts off the steps as my mom shows me how to slow dance. "One-two-three, one-two-three..." I can do it as long as I look at my feet. Kim laughs. "You can't dance with your head down like that! You look *ridiculous!*"

"My feet won't listen," I say defensively.

Mom goes over to the stereo and changes the CD. "Your dad and I used to dance like this." Then she grabs Kim's hand. I sit on the sofa beside my grandmother, and we shriek with laughter as Mom spins Kim around the living room to a song from *Saturday Night Fever*. When it ends, Kim falls dramatically to the floor and does the splits. We applaud wildly.

"I thought you and dad went to different schools," I say, remembering their faded high school graduation pictures. My mom had long hair then, and my dad had a moustache. He looked like a bandit in an old western.

Mom smiles mysteriously. "The first time we met was at my grad."

"Sounds romantic," teases Kim.

Mom blushes. "Never mind," she says. "Come on, David. Try again."

I groan as Kim bounces up off the floor and drags me back to the center of the living room. We dance, and they all laugh at my imitation of John Travolta. Kim does it better, but then she's watched that movie at least twenty times and memorized all the dance routines.

"Show-off," I say to Kim.

"Oh, you're very good," says a deep voice from the doorway.

"Daddy," Kim shrieks. She runs over to give him a hug, happy that he's back from wherever he's been. I pick up the remote from the table beside the sofa and switch on the television.

"David," my mom says, disappointed. She shuts off the stereo.

"What? I want to watch TV." I flop down into the

armchair and flick through the channels.

"So did you find a suit?" Kim gladly tells my dad all the details. "You're lucky your grandmother got it for you."

"Yeah, I know." A game show contestant has to run through a floating obstacle course without getting knocked into the water by rotating paddles.

"It'll be a big night," he says. "Are your friends renting a limousine?"

"Yeah, but so what? It's not like I can chip in."

The contestant's timing is bad. A paddle whacks him, and he does a belly flop into the chilly water. My dad stares at me for a few seconds, and then leaves the room. Kim goes all quiet. Looking worried, she scrambles to sit beside Nai-nai.

"David," my mom whispers, after he disappears up the stairs. "He was just asking you a question."

"It was a stupid question," I say. It reminds me that I won't have any money to take Christine out afterwards.

CHAPTER 17

I'm working harder at being a good employee. My voice is more cheerful and polite on the phone. My smile is more welcoming to everyone who comes to the desk. I make sure I do whatever Mark asks me to do because I don't have the money. If I'm good, will he forgive me for something he doesn't know about?

"I am not a crook." My history teacher said those were famous words from a former American president. Well, I'm not a crook either. I tried to give the money back, I really did. But my mom was not in a generous mood this morning.

"What do you need it for?" she asked. She was flipping through the newspaper, relaxing before she went to bed. I finished breakfast and put off asking for money until the very last minute, hoping to get it and make a fast getaway. She had a look on her face that stopped me from saying I wanted to play the hockey pool. It was only a few bucks, but I might as well have been asking for a thousand.

I just want to give back the money that I accidentally put into my pocket, and then spent on movies with the guys. "The guys are going out." I mumbled whatever popped into my head. Whatever was believable. "Craig keeps asking why I don't do anything anymore."

"Well, you can ask your friends to come here."

"It's not the same. And I don't want them to know we don't have any money." That's the truth, but the truth doesn't always get me what I want.

"It's only temporary, and you don't need to spend money to have fun." She was trying to make me feel better, but it didn't work.

"You should've told Dad that."

"That's enough," she snapped. "We have to pull out of this together. Having a bad attitude won't help. Yes, your dad made a serious mistake, but you can learn from this, too."

Yeah, well, I wouldn't do something that stupid. I knew better than to say it out loud when she was in that mood, so I shoved my chair back and got up.

"We have a lot of movies here, or they can bring one and you can watch it together." Her tone was apologetic, but I didn't want to talk anymore.

Shame poked me in the gut. I knew she'd give me the money if she could. It wasn't her fault.

Then my dad came into the kitchen.

I hate him.

At work, I try to keep a cheerful face as one mother thanks me for helping her choose a music book. I ring up the sale, carefully put the money into the drawer, and count out her change. I can barely walk by the rack, the scene of the crime.

Craig enters and comes up to the desk. "Hey, David. What are you doing after work?"

I sigh. "I don't know. Why?" I grab a bunch of invoices and focus on re-organizing them.

"Me, Andrew, and Todd are going to the mall this afternoon. Nathalie said she'd probably be there with Sandra and Christine."

"To do what?"

"Hang out." He lowers his voice to a whisper. "Gonna

find out if Nathalie has a date for the grad."

Going to the mall means I have to have money. It'd be nice to treat Christine to a soft drink or an ice cream or something. But that's just a dream.

"You don't want to see Christine?"

"Hey, I'm busy. I have other things to do, too, you know." I say it sharper than I intended.

Craig backs off. "Hey, okay, just thought you'd want to go." He looks puzzled.

"Sorry. It's my parents." It's all I'm willing to admit.

"That's cool. Okay. See ya." He heads off to his lesson.

Why am I taking it out on Craig? I don't know what to feel, but I'm scared my friends will find out we're poor and think I'm a loser. Dad's the one who caused this mess, but Mom won't give me any money. It was only a few bucks. If I was getting paid for this job, I'd make that back in a couple of hours. What's the big deal?

I fling the pile of invoices down. They land with a big smack and scatter over the desk. A couple of people look over at me. Why can't they mind their own business? I gather up the invoices, arrange them into a neat pile, and place them in the box marked "Accounting".

A boy comes up and puts a music book on the counter. He hands me twenty bucks. I stare at the money like it's a sign. I put it down beside the cash register and give him the change, just a few cents. Emily doesn't mind if the cash is out by a few cents. The boy takes the music book and leaves.

I take a quick look around to see if anyone's watching. I'm feeling guilty, and I haven't done anything wrong yet. Nobody notices because there's isn't anyone left to see. Everyone has either left or gone into the studios.

The twenty dollar bill is on the desk beside the cash register. It's been in purses, wallets, and was probably tucked into the back pocket of the kid who just bought the music book. I put my hand on top, covering it. It's smooth, new—probably came from a stack of bills wrapped with a paper strip like the ones bank robbers steal in the movies. The corners stick out from under my fingers. I slowly slide my fingers along the desk, into my palm. It doesn't make a noise and nobody, especially me, hears or sees it disappear into my fist.

And then I close the cash register.

* * *

People flow through the glass doors into the mall. It's a cloudy day, so everyone's here to bask in the warm glow of the fluorescent lights. I scan the crowd of mothers, squealing brats, gangs of giggling thirteen-year-old girls; people in a hurry and people just passing time.

Goose bumps break out all over my arms, and the air-conditioning sends a chill up my spine. A heavy, hollow feeling spreads from the pit of my stomach to my fingers and toes, but it's too late to turn back. The lonely twenty dollar bill is a weight in my pocket. I don't belong here. Sales are meant for people who have money; people who want to spend, not save. I push my way further inside.

Craig said he'd meet me near the information booth. I head in that direction, and see a sight that takes my breath away. Six shiny new cars and trucks are on display; a harmony of gleaming chrome, spoilers, leather seats, and horsepower. Craig's sitting behind the wheel of a black convertible with cream-colored seats. He waves, and I head over.

"Hey," he says, with one eye in the rearview mirror. "Do I look good in this?"

"Yeah," I say. "It's you. Where is everybody?"

"Eating." He gets out of the car, and we linger for awhile, getting behind the driver's seat of every car. Craig whistles at the sticker price, while I avoid looking at it. What's the point? Then we head to the food court.

I can hear the food court before we get there. The noise is like one loud stomach growl. There are lineups everywhere. Trays bang on stainless-steel counters, cash registers ring, and hundreds of people talk at once. People balance food, bags, and babies as they hunt for a table in a space designed to make shoppers feel like they're on a picnic.

Andrew's waiting in line for pizza. He spots us, and then points to the middle of the hungry mob. Christine and the others are sitting at a long table. Seeing her lifts my spirits, and I head straight for the empty seat beside her. She looks glad to see me, too, and I feel a twinge of happiness.

"Is anyone else going to eat?" Craig asks, looking at Nathalie.

"Yeah, but we haven't decided yet," says Christine.

"I think I'll have a hamburger," says Nathalie.

"Sounds good to me," says Craig, and they walk off together.

Christine turns to me. "Did you hear the latest about the band for prom?" she asks.

I shake my head.

"It's a local band," she says.

A moan of disappointment goes around the table.

"We'll still have a good time," I say, careful not to mention anything about going out afterwards.

Nathalie comes back alone and empty handed. She's beaming. "Craig's treating me to lunch," she says to the other girls, as she sits down. "He's so sweet."

I should've known Craig would resort to bribery. The things he'll do to get a date. Now I'll have to buy Christine lunch, or risk looking like a cheapskate. I stick my hand into the pocket of my jeans and feel the twenty-dollar bill for confidence. It's just a loan, I tell myself. "Christine, I want to treat you to lunch, too." I stand up.

"You don't have to," she says, and slides out of her seat. "I have my own money." With the other girls watching and waiting for my answer, that's when I know I have to.

"No, I really want to. How about souvlaki?"

Christine hesitates, then smiles and says, "Okay."

When I insist, she also agrees to fries and a soft drink. I head to the lineup at the souvlaki stand. There's no turning back now.

When I get back to the table with the tray, Christine happily shares her fries with me. I eat slowly, digesting the fact that I am a crook. I can barely taste the thick-cut fries.

"How do you like working at Le Grenier de la musique?" Christine asks.

"It's okay," I mumble.

"I'm looking for a part-time job for the summer," she says. "I think it's great you're getting paid to work in something you love. You're lucky."

"Yeah," I reply. I avoid looking at her, glancing through the crowd around the food court, when a familiar figure appears and disappears. My heart leaps into my mouth. Is that Mark? Is he hunting me down? The shape of the crowd thickens, then thins out. The man breaks through, pushing a baby carriage. It's not him.

Christine nudges me, and I almost jump out of the chair.

"David, do you want to go?" she asks shyly. I look around the table. Everyone's waiting for my answer.

I blink and stammer. "Uh… Well, I don't know. You?"

"I wouldn't mind seeing a movie."

My stomach does a flip, and my heart sinks. I stare at her while searching for an answer. "I don't know," I mumble. "I told my mom I'd do stuff for her."

"Do you want to call her?" Christine pulls a cell phone out of her purse.

"No!" I say, a bit too loudly. Startled, she leans away from me. The whole gang is looking and listening. "I mean, she's not home."

Christine nods as if she understands, but looks disappointed.

I could kick myself.

Everyone agrees with Craig's suggestion to head straight to the theatre to see if they can catch the next show. I follow them out of the food court, trying to look interested in the chatter, but my disappointment absorbs the excitement around me. They happily climb into Craig and Francine's cars, and wave as they drive out of the parking lot. I wave back with a stupid grin across my face.

Life sucks.

CHAPTER 18

Lunch time in the school cafeteria sounds like an orchestra tuning up. Kitchen workers bang pots and pans and rattle dishes as they serve up whatever was defrosted that morning. Chairs scrape the floor. Boys whoop and holler. Girls chatter and giggle.

Cacophony. That's the word. But it's not loud enough to block out the conversation at my table.

Nathalie said yes to Craig, and now the guys are seriously talking about renting a limo. I sit quietly at the end of the table and pull out my lunch, hoping nobody asks me to join in.

"Man, we gotta get the Range Rover Sport," Mick says. "It's so cool."

"Or a Hummer," says Craig. "Now that's style."

"I'm a Lincoln Navigator kind of guy," Bruno says. "Elegant and classy." He's writing names and numbers on a napkin. "Hey, David, you in, or what?"

I shrug, and take a huge bite of my chicken sandwich so that I can't answer.

"Come on, David," Craig says. "It's cheaper if there's more of us."

Not if I don't have any money to begin with. I shrug.

"Don't get a stretch," Andrew says. He's been walking on air since Francine said yes. "Regular one's cheaper."

"Nah, stretch is better," Bruno replies. "More room, and there's a mini-bar."

"David," Craig says. "How are you going to get to the grad? Don't you want to pick up Christine in style?"

I wash down the sandwich with water before answering. "I don't think she cares."

"All the girls care," says Bruno.

"Nah," says Andrew. "They only care about the dress."

"How do you know?" Craig asks.

"My sister said so."

"Whatever," says Bruno. "Come on, David, it's only a few bucks."

"Stop bugging me!" I shove my chair back and stand up. "Do whatever you want! Ask someone else!"

"Whoa, okay." Bruno looks at me bug-eyed. "Don't get pissed about it."

They're all staring at me.

"Screw you," I say to all of them. I have to get away before I say something I'll regret later. Scooping up what's left of my sandwich and water, I dump it into the garbage can and get out of the cafeteria. Out in the hallway, I take a couple of deep breaths, filling my lungs with the aroma of macaroni and cheese. What's the matter with me? Why am I taking it out on my friends?

Craig follows me as I head down the hall. "What's wrong? Why'd you get so mad?"

"I don't want to talk about it."

"Something going on at home?" He catches up to me and lowers his voice to a whisper. "Is it that girl we saw your dad with?"

"Leave me alone." I walk faster, but Craig's a stubborn guy.

"Come on, man, you can talk to me. When my parents' divorce got bad, you listened."

"Why do we have to spend so much money? The

tickets to the grad cost enough. We just have to get there and have fun. That's it!"

Craig looks at me in confusion. "What's the problem? You're working."

"Yeah, but I don't get paid." It slipped out. I'm so embarrassed, I can't look at him.

"Why would you work for free? It's not like Mark runs a charity. How come he's not paying you?"

"So I can get free guitar lessons," I mumble, hoping he doesn't hear it.

"Oh, so why didn't you say so?"

He makes it sound like it's so easy. Sometimes there's no answer to simple questions. "You don't know what it's like."

"Hey, whaddya mean I don't know?" Craig looks offended. "My parents' divorce was awful. They fought about money all the time."

"Then how come you have money to spend now?"

"My mom pays me to do stuff around the house. It's not like I steal it. I earn it, and I can do what I want with it."

I wince at his comment.

"So where'd you get the money to buy Christine lunch?" I hate that he has a good memory.

When I don't answer, he looks scared. "Seriously, man. Where'd you get the money?"

"I took it," I whisper back. I take quick look around to make sure nobody heard. It's the second lunch period. The juniors are in their classes, and middle grades and seniors have disappeared to enjoy their brief hour of freedom.

He looks me in the eye and says hopefully, "From your mom?"

The consequences would be less severe if that was the truth. "Le Grenier." I mumble, but Craig hears me loud and clear.

"Are you kidding me? *You stole it?* How could you do something so stupid?"

"Hey, for a guy who's running a gambling ring, you shouldn't be so sanctimonious."

"At least everyone knows what they're in for, and it's not like I skim any off the top for myself."

That's true. I wouldn't have joined if I thought he pocketed any of the money.

"I don't want to lose my job."

"Does Mark suspect?"

"No!" I'm annoyed that Craig thinks I'd have been careless enough to arouse Mark's suspicion. But I was stupid enough to do it in the first place.

"You have to put it back."

"With what? You think I didn't already think of that? My mom won't give me any money."

"How much did you take?" he asks quietly.

"Forty bucks."

He reaches into his pocket and pulls out some bills. "I got twenty." He hands it to me, but I jerk my hand back as if he's on fire.

"What? I can't pay you back, and I can't spring for the limo either."

"You got any other ideas?"

If I'm really good and don't do it again, Mark will never find out. If he does, then I could say some kid stole the books. I know these are bad ideas, and I'd have to live with the guilt.

Salvation is in his hand. I take it.

"Listen," Craig says, pretending to search for something in his pockets. "The limo's a crazy idea. I don't want to cram into a car with six other people, mini-bar or not. My mom already said I can borrow her car, so how about if I drive you and Christine?"

My throat tightens, and I nod. Just when I'm feeling like crap, as if there's no way out of the hole I dug for myself, my best friend hands me a lifeline.

And I'm not talking about the money.

CHAPTER 19

The answer's so simple, I can't believe I didn't think of it before. D'oh!

I'm lucky to have a friend who wants to help, but all we did was split my problem in half. Instead of owing Le Grenier forty bucks, I owe twenty to Le Grenier and twenty to Craig. Bottom line: I'm still in the hole forty bucks.

Then it hits me: Craig's mother pays him for doing things around the house. If he can do it, so can I. My parents can't pay me, but someone else can.

Eureka! It's the best idea I've had so far.

It'll be a piece of cake. There's always things that need fixing or cleaning. I've helped my parents inside and outside the house my whole life. I'm a pro. It's about time I got paid for it.

On the way home, I start noticing things on my street that I've never noticed before, like the Christmas lights hanging off the roof of the house on the corner. Weeds are popping up in the garden next door. The garage across the street is packed with who-knows-what. Maybe the guy would hire someone to make space so he can park his van in it. People are busy. They'd probably be happy to hire someone like me to help.

Might as well start ringing some doorbells. With all the work I can see, I could make enough money before Saturday to cover what I owe Le Grenier and Craig, and still have enough to take Christine out on prom night.

I take a quick peek at my reflection in a car window.

Hair. Check.

Face clean. Check.

Zits. Too many.

"Hi," I say. My nice, friendly reflection smiles back at me. "Do you need help around the house?"

Who wouldn't hire me?

I walk up to the house with the dangly Christmas lights and ring the doorbell. After a few seconds, a blond middle-aged lady wearing an apron opens the door, releasing the smell of freshly baked cookies. Maybe she'll pay me in cookies. That'd be okay, just this once.

"Yes?"

"Hi," I say. "I'm, uh… David. I live down the street, in that house over there." I point it out, hoping she'll recognize it. She does. Well, it's not as if it was built yesterday. "I was wondering if you were looking to hire someone to do some work, like maybe take down the Christmas lights?"

"Ohh," she says, in an apologetic tone. "No, not really."

"You don't want to take down the lights? Or maybe fix them?" I ask hopefully, and point to the dangling string on the corner of the roof.

She laughs and shakes her head. "My husband takes care of it. Or at least he should." Then she adds, "Hey, I'm baking cookies to raise money for my daughter's elementary school. I don't suppose you want to buy some?"

"Sorry," I reply. "They smell really good, but I don't have any money."

"Okay," she laughs again, and adds. "Good luck."

Luck is exactly what I need. Nobody was home at the garden full of weeds, and at the house with the garage full of stuff, the guy acts as if I'm trying to rob him.

"Whaddya mean, clean out my garage?" His black, beady eyes examine me as if he'll need to point me out in a police lineup later.

"Or maybe help organize it?" I put on a big, friendly smile, and try not to look scared, which I am. He's a big guy and doesn't smell too good.

"I know where everything is. I don't need a teenager" —he says the word "teenager" like he's learning a foreign language— "to tell me how to organize my life." When he shuts the door, I'm glad I'm not working for him.

There's no answer at the house next door, or the one across the street. I might have to rethink my strategy. Maybe that last guy was insulted because I said his garage was a mess. One person's mess is another person's treasure chest. Like the toys in Kim's room; useless to me, gold to her. I should just let people decide what they want done.

A silver Acura sedan cuts across the sidewalk in front of me, into a driveway, and parks. The driver's door swings open, and Dr. Yip eases himself out with a grunt. As he steadies himself and stands up, he notices me and waves.

"Hey, David," says Dr. Yip, with his usual friendly smile. "How're you doing?"

"Okay," I reply. Dr. Yip and his wife have been neighbors for as long as I can remember. All of their kids graduated from university and moved out. He's been retired for years, and spends most of his time raising money for charity. Sometimes I see pictures of him and his wife in the newspaper at some fancy party that costs two hundred dollars a ticket. You gotta have money to go to parties like that. Lots of money. Yeah.

"Hey, Dr. Yip," I say, walking up the smooth black asphalt. "I'm, uh, thinking of starting my own job for the summer. Working for people."

"Good for you," he says, shutting the car door. A honk and a flicker of the headlights confirm the door's locked.

"Is there anything you need help with?"

He looks at me. "Like what?" We glance at the brick house, windows gleaming under the sunshine. A pretty rock garden outlines one side of the greenest grass on the block. There's not a speck of garbage in sight or a runaway Christmas decoration. Not a hint of anything that needs work.

"I can't hire you to do the gardening. My wife says I need the exercise." Dr. Yip shrugs.

"I can do a lot of things," I say, desperate not to let it go. "I help out at home all the time."

"Well, what can you do for me?"

"Uh... Well, if there's something you don't want to do." I don't want to risk insulting him, like I might've done with the last guy.

"Sorry, I'd like to help you out, but I can't think of anything."

He's turning away, and I'm frantically looking at his house, the yard, the garage, when I suddenly see it.

"I can wash your car!" The Acura's not that dirty, but it's not really clean either.

Dr. Yip stops and turns back. "How much do you want?"

I hadn't even thought about that. Should I ask for minimum wage? When the school had a car wash to raise money for the grad, we only charged five bucks. It won't take long anyway. That might be the way to go. I just need to wash four cars, and I'll be able to pay Craig back.

"Five?" I ask hopefully.

"Sure," he says. "Want to do it now? I'll show you where everything is."

In no time, I rinse the car and get a bucket full of soapy water. As I'm soaping one side of the car, I hear Dr. Yip say hello to Nai-nai. She walks across the lawn, to the small hedge that separates our houses.

They're still chatting when I finish rinsing off the car. I coil the hose and hang it back on the hook in the garage. Then I empty the bucket of dirty water into the sewer. Using a chamois I found on a shelf, I dry off the car, carefully checking the windows for streaks.

"Hey, David," Dr. Yip suddenly calls out in Chinese. "Your grandmother says you're working for free!"

What? My Chinese isn't that good, but I hope he didn't say what I thought he just said.

"Ah, David," says Nai-nai. "You do not need to ask for money."

What is she saying? "Nai-nai, I'm not asking for it, I'm working for it," I say, hoping she misunderstood.

She shakes her head and waves her hand as if she's shooing a fly. That isn't a good sign. I leave the chamois on the roof of the car and quickly head over to them.

Dr. Yip reaches into his back pocket and pulls out his wallet. Nai-nai urges him to put it back.

"I'd like to pay you, David, but she won't let me," Dr. Yip says, chuckling. If it was any other time, I'd laugh. It looks like they're arm-wrestling. Nai-nai has a good grip on his arm and is trying to grab his wallet. Dr. Yip isn't putting up much of a fight, and I'm not too happy about that.

"We are good friends. Good neighbors. You do not pay," Nai-nai insists.

As soon as she says that, I know I'm doomed. If I ask him to pay, she'll lose face, and will feel that I'm being disrespectful towards her. And he can't pay me out of respect for her wishes. There's nothing I can do but watch as Dr. Yip slowly and cheerfully loses the battle.

"It's okay," I say with a sigh, as Dr. Yip holds his hands up in surrender. "This one's on me."

CHAPTER 20

"Hi, David," says Mark. He's leaning against the reception desk as if he's waiting for me. Does he know? Did he figure it out?

"Hi, Mark!" I say, forcing enthusiasm into my voice.

Putting the money back is the only way out, and the right thing to do. Even though Mark doesn't know that I took the money, I hurt him, and he doesn't deserve to be treated that way. Maybe I shouldn't give up on making money by washing cars so soon. I may have lost five dollars with Dr. Yip, but Nai-nai doesn't know everybody in the neighborhood.

At least this part will be over soon.

I walk behind the desk, noticing the cash register drawer isn't closed tight. I stare at it, taking my time stowing my guitar under the desk. When Mark disappears into his office, I pull open the drawer.

It's empty.

Of course. He didn't put the money in yet.

"Can you sweep the front steps?" I jump at the sound of Mark's voice, and the hairs on the back of my neck stand up. My hand's in the empty till. He's in the doorway to his office at the back of the room. My mouth opens, but

I can't make a sound, so I nod.

I go to the closet, take out the broom, and head outside. The broom kicks up small clouds of dust as I whip it around, sweeping as fast as I can. The iron railings ring out in baritones as the broom bumps against them. I need to put the money back while the store's empty. If anyone's around, there's more of a chance that I'll get caught. Is getting caught putting money back in the till as bad as taking it out? Would Mark see it as an act of honesty or cowardice? If I can do it, I'll be halfway home.

The reception area is empty when I go back inside. I toss the broom back in the closet and quickly head to the desk. I slowly press the "No Sale" key to open the drawer, hoping it won't make any noise, but when it clicks, the cash register whirrs, and there's a little ding as the drawer pops open. My heart's pounding, and I take a quick look over my shoulder to Mark's office. All's quiet.

The cash is in the till.

I stick my hand into my pocket and pull out the twenty Craig gave me. I unfold the bill and slip it into the till when a deep voice asks, "What're you doing?"

Mark's looking at me. Actually, he's looking at the twenty, which is halfway in. Or, from his point of view, halfway out of the drawer.

I freeze. My mouth opens before my brain has a chance to figure out what to say. I force the words out. "Um... I... Someone bought a book."

He looks at me. "There isn't anyone here. I didn't hear anyone come in."

"They left." I stretch my lips into a grin. This isn't going well.

Keeping his eyes on me, Mark walks over to the desk. "Did you ring in the sale?" The twenty dollar bill is stuck to my fingers. "How about we count the float together," he says, and begins to take the money from the cash register.

* * *

I can't explain it, but I have to and Mark's waiting for an answer. The cushion on the chair is thin, and the hard metal underneath it is making me uncomfortable. Emily's at reception, so Mark and I can have a talk in his office.

He doesn't look mad, but there are deep creases between his bushy eyebrows. I've never seen him angry, but I don't know what to expect, so I'm scared. My hands are between my knees to stop the shaking, but my feet are jumpy.

"David," he says. I stare at the edge of the old wood office desk, nicks and scratches creating a haphazard design. "Do you want to tell me what you were doing?"

"Just putting money back," I say as calmly as I can. He looked relieved and puzzled when the entire fifty-dollar float was there. It's the twenty dollar bill lying on the desk between us that he cannot understand.

"Why?"

I'm waiting for an earthquake to swallow me up, or for someone to choke on one of those free candies at the reception desk so I can run out, save their life, and be a hero. Mark would be so grateful to me for saving him from a big lawsuit that he'd forget about asking what I was doing. I stare at the phone, praying someone will call to say something drastic has happened to someone in my family or in his, so he'll know that life is precious and should not be wasted on twenty bucks.

I should have known that.

"Someone bought a book."

"When?"

I shrug.

He sighs. "David, twenty dollars is not a lot of money. I'm concerned about your actions."

What would he say if he knew I stole twice that much? Would I be in twice as much trouble? "Someone did buy a book."

"That's interesting, because I took a stock count the other day and noticed that a couple of music books were missing."

I stop breathing.

"David." It's painful for me to raise my eyes from the edge of the desk and look at him. He doesn't look mad, but it feels as if he can see right through me. "Tell me what happened."

It spills out. "It's my dad's fault!"

He frowns. One of his eyebrows rises up to listen.

I tell him everything. I don't mean to, but it all comes out in one long piece.

"He lost so much money gambling! My mom works long shifts most of the week, and if I didn't get a job, I'd have to give up guitar lessons. My sister had to give up dance lessons. And what are my friends going to think if I can't even afford to go to a movie?"

It all comes out like a train that's fallen off the track. Only the first car hits something, but all the other cars behind it fall, too. Mark listens without saying a word.

When I finish talking, I'm breathless, as if I just skated a hockey rink end-to-end.

The silence between us is heavy. His mouth is clenched, and he looks a little sad. Whether or not I made things worse by confessing, I don't know, but I feel lighter. A fog has been lifted. I can't do anything about what happens now.

Mark's silent for a few moments. Then he clears his throat. "Since you tried to put the money back, I'm sure you know what you did was wrong."

It's gonna be okay. He's letting me off the hook.

Then he sighs. "But, David, stealing is a serious crime. It's not just the money. The trust between an employer and employee is a delicate thing. I just don't know if I can trust you anymore."

A lump in my throat keeps me from crying out and begging him not to fire me. It's the worst thing that can happen.

    "I'll have to call your parents," he says.

    I was wrong.

CHAPTER 21

Mark hangs up the phone. "Your mother wants you to go straight home."

"Am I fired?" I ask, even though I know. I ask to make sure I'm not imagining the trouble I'm in.

"Yes." The edges of his eyes are weighed down by his decision.

"Does that mean I can't take lessons, even if I could pay for them?" I want to be brave about this, but my voice is trembling.

"You can take lessons anytime you want. David, you're talented, and I enjoy being your instructor, but you just can't work for me anymore," Mark says, slowly shaking his head.

I nod. The only words that stick in my mind are *I can't work for him anymore.* I stand up. There's only one door. I go through it and walk past Emily, the other instructors, and all the people in the waiting area. Even though the office door was closed, they know. I can feel it.

Their fingers are pointing at me as I walk by.

Emily gets up from the chair as I grab my guitar from beneath the desk.

"Hey, David," she says, as I'm about to leave. "Are you

taking your lesson now?" She looks puzzled.

Shaking my head, I sling the bag over my back.

Mark is standing on the other side of the counter. "Emily, can you sit here for a few minutes, so I can call Nancy and ask her to come in?"

"Sure," she says. Emily shoots a concerned look at me. "Everything okay?"

I hear Mark whisper to her. What did he tell her? That I'm a crook?

"David," says Mark. "Take care."

I can't look at him, so I nod. Without saying goodbye to Emily or any of the other instructors, I hurry out the door and almost collide with a girl and her violin case.

I'll never come back, even if I could pay for lessons.

Right now, I just want to get out of here as fast as I can. After unlocking my bike, I swing my leg over the seat, jump on, and pedal hard.

It's still early, so there aren't many cars on the road. Saturday papers lie on doorsteps. The rough sound of a gas lawn mower rumbles through the air, like thunder in the distance. A poodle is pulling on its leash, taking a small girl for a walk. I lean forward, pressing hard on the pedals, racing to escape myself and my problems. I take the long way home to burn off a sudden burst of energy, barely stopping at stop signs. One quick glance down an empty street, and I take off again. Soon, I'm not even stopping at all. It feels too good, the wind, the burning in my legs and lungs. I want to get as far away as I can from Mark, Emily, and those stupid music books.

There's nothing but a smooth stretch of asphalt before me. I pedal as if my life depends on getting to the end of it. I whip past a couple of kids on their bikes. The street slopes down and I let gravity pull me forward. I slow down to make a right turn at a corner, but not slow enough.

The turn is too wide, or I'm not paying enough attention. I lose control and swerve to avoid crashing into a parked car. I lean too far, skid, and fall over. My arms fly out and my body slaps the pavement. Air rushes out of my lungs. I feel and hear the crunch as my helmet makes contact with the street. The street becomes the sky, trees and houses are whirling around me. Suddenly, I'm afraid my bike will fall on me. I don't know where it is because I can't figure out which way is up. Finally, I stop rolling, but it feels like my brain is still spinning.

A man races over and kneels beside me. His dark, round face is anxious and concerned. "Hey, kid. You okay?"

I don't feel anything until he asks. Suddenly, my arms are burning and my bones ache. He kneels beside me and holds his hand in front of my face. "How many fingers?"

It takes a couple of seconds for my mind and mouth to connect. "Two." I want to get up, but I can't.

Oh, God. I broke my back. *I'll be in a wheelchair for the rest of my life.*

"Good. Don't get up too fast," he says. "That was quite a tumble. Good thing you're wearing a helmet."

"I can't get up," I say, fear rising in my throat.

"It's your guitar. Roll onto your side and sit up."

I do as he says, with his help. He lifts the case up over my head and shows it to me. It hangs limp in his hands. I slowly unzip the nylon case, afraid of what I will find. The guitar is barely in one piece. It's cracked and splintered, held together by the strings and the case. My stupidity not only lost me my job, it also broke my guitar.

I sit on the street and cry.

CHAPTER 22

Stupid, stupid, stupid.

I roll down the street and up the driveway to my house at a crawl. The bike survived the crash with fewer scratches than I did. After I managed to stand up, it took a few deep breaths to stop the shaking. That guy offered to give me first aid, but I refused out of pride and embarrassment. I thanked him, then stifled a moan as I lifted my leg over the crossbar and put my foot on the pedal. I just wanted to get away, again, from a situation that was all my fault. My hands are scraped, my pants are torn, and my knee is bleeding, but they don't take my mind off the fact that I was fired from my first job. I coast into the garage, brake, and wince as I get off. I lean the bike against the cement block wall and, on my way out, drop the helmet into the garbage can.

Wouldn't you know it, as soon as I step inside the house, my grandmother and Kim turn from the television and look at me. They both gasp. Kim squeals loud enough to bring my mom in from whatever she was doing.

Mom's eyes bug out when she sees me. "What happened?"

I'm running over the conversation with Mark in my

mind when she rushes over.

"Look at your knee!" She gives me a quick medical check up. "Did you fall off your bike? Were you wearing your helmet?"

I nod, relieved, glad that her attention is diverted. When I slip the guitar bag from my back, the full impact of what might have happened registers in her mind and her face.

"Did you get hit by a car?" she asks, in horror.

"No. I took a corner too fast and fell." I swallow a painful moan and slowly limp up the stairs, trying to ignore the sting of my injuries while discovering new aches and pains. In my room, I let the bag crumple to the floor, then stagger over to my bed and fall on it.

Bathroom cupboards open and slam shut. "David!" my mom calls out. "Come to the bathroom. You have to clean those cuts and scrapes."

I groan.

I can't get up.

I have to get up.

Slowly rolling off the side of the bed, I manage to steady myself on my feet and stagger over the bathroom a few steps down the hall. Kim's standing there, wide-eyed and no doubt eager to hear what happened. I walk past her and ease myself down onto the yellow bathmat hanging over the side of the tub. Boxes of bandages, cotton, gauze, a bottle of iodine, and a tube of Polysporin are waiting on the counter.

"You're lucky nothing's broken," Mom says.

"Yeah." I close my eyes. The stinging wounds on my body are a distraction. Mom looks so worried that I'm actually hoping she forgot about Mark's phone call.

"Let me see your knee," she commands, pulling at the tear in my jeans.

"No, it's okay. I can do it." Grunting like an old man, I manage to pull up the torn pant leg. What skin that hasn't been scraped off is hanging in bits, clumped with dirt and blood.

"Ugh," I say. Just looking at it makes it more painful.

"You have to clean it before we bandage it," she says, with nurse-like efficiency.

"Get outta here," I tell Kim, who's watching the whole thing like it's an episode of *CSI*.

"After you change your pants, come downstairs," Mom says. "We have to talk."

"Just tell me what you want to say. I don't want to go downstairs. Everything hurts. My side hurts when I breathe." I take a deep breath and wince, but she's not in the mood to give me a lot of sympathy.

"Take your time," she says, and leaves, closing the door behind her to Kim's protests.

I slowly peel off my socks and pants, dropping them onto the floor. Then I turn around and put my feet into the tub. I turn on the taps, adjusting them so that the water's bearable, and carefully splash water over my palms and onto my knee. It stings, and I clamp my mouth tight to stifle a groan, but the pain's nothing compared to when I add soap to the wound.

I carefully pat every cut and scrape dry with a clean towel. It doesn't look so bad once all the guck is gone. I guess I'll live. I put some Polysporin on, and then tape a folded piece of gauze over it. I clean the palms of my hands and elbows in the same way. When I'm all sterilized and bandaged, I let out a sigh of relief. It's over.

Almost.

I make my way back to my room, one agonizing step at a time, and collapse onto the bed from the sheer weight of my problem. I know what Mom wants: an explanation.

I don't move for a couple of minutes. Falling off my bike and being that close to death didn't erase Mark's phone call from her mind. I'm going to have to face it.

I reach out and grab a pair of jeans hanging on the back of a chair. My muscles ache with every move I make, and it takes a few minutes to change. Going down the stairs is as painful as going up. Mom's in the living room. Nai-nai and Kim have disappeared, but I'm pretty sure Kim is within hearing distance.

"Can you fix them?" I ask, giving my mother the torn jeans.

She examines the flap of material on the leg and sighs, "I don't think so." She folds them and puts them beside her on the sofa. "David, I want to know what happened with Mark. Did you steal from him?"

"No!" The look on her face says she doesn't believe me.

"The first time was an accident," I blurt out.

"The first time?" Her eyes widen in shock and anger.

I suddenly remember that Mark thinks it only happened once.

"How can you steal by accident?" The question is as hard as the tone of her voice.

Somehow I get through the whole story. After I tell her that Mark only caught me trying to put the money back, the look on her face softens just a bit.

"Well, it's good that you tried to put the money back, but it doesn't take away the fact that you stole it in the first place. Twice."

I don't say anything and hope that since I tried to right a wrong, she'll go easier on me.

"Stealing is serious."

"I won't do it again."

"The first time wasn't really a mistake. You could have put the money back then." She's right. It's the cold hard truth. "I'm so disappointed in you."

Her last sentence slices right through me.

She crosses her arms and bites down on her lower lip as if she's trying hard not to yell at me, or cry. We sit there for a few moments without saying anything. I never thought how she'd feel knowing someone thinks her son's a thief. I suddenly realize I'm not the only one who can never go back to Le Grenier de la musique and face Mark again.

"David, you have to be punished," Mom says. Her voice is as expressionless as her face.

"Mark already fired me," I quickly remind her. "It's bad enough as it is. And my guitar got smashed!"

"I know, but you have to understand that you're not the only one who suffered from your actions. You broke Mark's trust, and it reflects on the entire family."

"I know! I said I won't do it again!" I blew my only chance to get free guitar lessons and trashed my guitar in an accident. How much worse can it get?

"You're grounded."

I stare at her, waiting for her to finish the sentence, to add some kind of explanation because it just doesn't make any sense.

She doesn't. Maybe I didn't understand.

"Grounded? The grad is two weeks away." Maybe she means just the weekend.

"You can't go to the grad."

"What?" I explode and leap off the sofa. "That's not fair! I already got fired!"

"Yes, because Mark caught you," her voice is firm. She looks me in the eye, and I know she's not going to change her mind. "You knew it was wrong, but you did it anyway. Especially the second time. Going to the grad is a reward you don't deserve."

The anger and frustration stewing up inside of me boil over. "Why are you doing this to me? Dad screwed up big, and you forgave him! I make one little mistake, and I can't go to the grad! It's *his* fault we don't have money for anything!"

Without waiting to hear another word, I race back up to my room, taking the stairs two at a time. Pulling open the closet door, I yank out a brown plastic suit bag. Then I go back to the stairway and throw it down the stairs.

"Here! I won't need this anymore. You can get Nai-nai's money back." Without waiting to hear Mom's reply, I storm back to my room, slamming the door shut. The jury of guitar greats look down at me, unsympathetic. "Don't judge me!" I rip the posters from the wall. Ragged pieces of thick, glossy paper fall like mutant snowflakes on the bed, the desk, and the floor.

The jury is out.

This whole thing is not my fault. It's the adults in this family who make my life complicated. What made me think I could take Christine to the prom?

Oh, no!

I have to tell Christine I can't go.

CHAPTER 23

"So," Craig leans up against the lockers and whispers, "did you put it back?"

A feeling of dread passes over me when I hear his voice. I managed to avoid him until now, and instead of going to the cafeteria, I had planned to eat my lunch alone outside the library, on a bench behind a bush. Yesterday, I spent the whole day in my room, angrily shoving pieces of poster into the garbage can, convinced it was Craig's fault I got caught. If he hadn't lent me the money, Mark never would have found out. But by the time I went to bed, I knew that no matter how I tried to spin the story, it was still my fault. Like Mom said, you can't *accidentally* steal anything.

"What happened to your hands?" Craig asks.

I hold up the palms of my hands so he can get a better look at the bandages. "Fell off my bike."

"How'd you do that?"

"Took a curve too fast."

He nods. "So? Did you do it?"

It's hard to face my best friend and tell him I screwed up again. I stare into my locker.

"Yeah," I say, "I put it back."

"Cool."

"I got caught. Mark fired me."

"Oh, crap."

"And I can't go to the grad."

"What?!"

Leaning my forehead against the locker, I close my eyes. "I don't know how to tell Christine."

The hall is crowded, and Christine's friends might accidentally overhear our conversation. Okay, I'm hoping one of them will hear and tell her so that I won't have to. If I'm really lucky, someone will tweet about it.

"You have to tell her soon, man. The longer you put it off, the worse it'll be."

Since when did Craig become an expert on dealing with girls? I look at him as if he just told me he's giving up drumming to bake cakes.

"How?" His last piece of advice cost me my job, so there's no way I'm going to do what he says.

He shrugs. "Just tell her."

"Oh, yeah," I snicker. "I can say 'Christine, I got caught stealing, so now my parents won't let me go to the grad.' Great idea."

"Say whatever you want, but tell her you can't go to the grad," says Craig. "Tell her your grandmother's in the hospital or something."

"My grandmother's not sick."

"For your information, Mr. Honesty, it's called a lie, which obviously you're not very good at."

"And you are?"

"Yeah." Craig looks smug about his hidden talent.

"No, you're not," I say, with a sneer.

"How would you know?" He looks pleased with himself. "You've never caught me."

I look at my friend and wonder if he's lying right now. But he has a good point. It sounds a whole lot better than telling Christine the truth.

* * *

If I'm right, Christine has a free period. I'm not ready to tell her, but the more I think about it, the more Craig seems right. The longer I put it off, the worse it will be. Telling her the night before the grad would be social suicide.

Sunlight beams in through stained-glass windows. The library is as quiet as a church, which is appropriate, since it used to be a church. I wander down one aisle, studying faces behind books and laptops, and peek into the book stacks.

Not there.

I've turned at the end and am headed down the other side when I spot her. She's sitting with a couple of friends, open books piled in front of them.

Christine sees me. She gives me a big smile and waves. Just seeing her makes me smile, until I remember why I'm looking for her. Her friends giggle when I ask Christine if we could talk privately. As we head into the stacks, one of them whispers, "Romeo."

Tall open metal shelves stuffed with books give the illusion of privacy. I peer through the books on either side of us to make sure we're alone. Christine's eyes are shining, and she's looking at me as if I'm her hero. It makes me think twice about what I'm about to do.

But I have to do it.

"Uh, Christine, I have some bad news." The smile disappears from her face, and she braces herself for whatever I'm going to say.

"It's, uh… It's Nai-nai, my grandmother," I whisper, afraid someone will hear me, and not because we're in the library. "She's not feeling well."

Christine's face melts into concern. It's working! I'm practically off the hook!

"What's wrong?" She sounds as if she really cares. I have to swallow a lump of guilt before I answer.

"She's been in and out of the hospital a lot lately."

"Oh, my God, your family must be so worried!" she whispers.

I put on a sad face and sigh. She puts her hand on my arm, and the warmth shoots straight to my face.

"Is she going to have surgery?"

"Um, we don't know yet." I haven't decided what my grandmother will be sick with. She has to be sick enough for me to explain why I can't go to the grad, but not so sick that she can't recover quickly. I decided on some mysterious old person's disease. "They're still running tests."

"What happened?" she asks.

"Well, like I said…"

Christine cuts me off. "To you. What happened to your hands?" She points to the bandages covering the palms of my hands.

I shrug. "Fell off my bike."

"Looks bad."

"It's just a scrape," I say bravely.

"Are her legs swelling?"

"No, my legs aren't swelling."

"Not you, your grandmother. That happened to my mom. It was so painful she could barely walk. It turned out to be a virus."

"Uh, no, she walks okay," I say, and quickly add, "but she's in bed most of the time."

"Do you think it's her heart?"

"Uh, no, we're pretty sure it's not that."

"How's her memory?"

"Good. I mean, as good as it can be for a seventy-eight-year-old."

"Cancer?" she whispers.

I shake my head, wondering when she's going to run out of diseases. "It's nothing life-threatening. We're not that worried about it." Christine frowns, and I quickly backtrack. "I mean, we have to be careful because of her age. And I just wouldn't feel right having a good time at the grad when she's in the hospital."

When she realizes what I'm saying, her face falls in disappointment. "But if it's not life-threatening…"

Craig's right. I'm lousy at this.

"My mom's worried, and I… I should be there to comfort her. My dad's working late a lot, and Kim's too young to help." I throw in a sigh and look sadly at the floor for effect because I can't look Christine in the eye.

I can feel her looking at me. The next few seconds are agonizing, until she finally says, "Of course you have to be with her. I'd do the same if it was my grandmother."

I sigh a little more heavily this time, mostly from relief. "Thanks, and I'm really sorry I can't go with you." I look at her because I mean it.

She nods and smiles, but looks as if she's thinking of something. I hold my breath, waiting for her to scream, "Liar!"

Suddenly, she leans forward and kisses me on the cheek.

I'm stunned, and for a moment I can hardly see. My eyes refocus; I'm looking at the books behind her. *Straight Talk* and *Living an Honest Life* are two of the titles on the shelf.

It figures I'd walk into the Sociology section to tell Christine a big lie. Too bad I didn't come here before I got into all this trouble. I wonder if there's a book on "How to Lie to Your Prom Date."

"So, you think you'll still go to the grad?" I ask, when I finally get my breath back.

"Yeah, I'll probably go with some friends. Not everyone has a date." She smiles as if everything's okay.

Suddenly, it hits me and sinks in. What have I done? I'll be missing the big night, celebrating graduation with my friends and Christine. I swallow my disappointment and say, "I'm glad you won't miss it because of me." And I really mean it.

"I wish you could go, too." The look on her face tells me she really means it. I watch her walk back to her friends. Then I slump against the bookshelves, mentally kicking myself, when a book falls off the shelf, hits my shoulder, and lands face-down on the floor. I pick it up and flip it over to read the title.

Little White Lies: How Small Things Lead to Big Disasters.

I should find my library card.

CHAPTER 24

The rest of the afternoon is a blur. All the classes blend into each other, and it feels as if the teachers are reading from the same script.

"Today, we're going to review what you need to know for the final exam. We'll take a look at *blah, blah, blah, blah, blah…*"

I can't go. Those words, and the disappointed look on Christine's face when I said them, haunt me. I try to wipe it out of my mind, but there are reminders everywhere.

Go to Grad For the Most Memorable Night of Your Life! screams one poster, one of many the grad committee taped onto the walls all over school. Those memories are now a hollow ache in my chest.

By the time I get home, my feet are dragging. I'm still hurting from the accident, but it feels worse today, and I can barely make it up the stairs. Once I get in my room, I fall on the bed and stare at the bare walls. Pale outlines mark the memory of what happened that awful afternoon.

I'll lie here forever. There's nothing for me outside my room, outside this house. I have no life. Nothing, absolutely nothing is going to make me want to get off my bed.

"David!" Kim shouts from downstairs. "Supper's

ready!"

Except that. A guy's gotta eat. Smells like ribs, one of my favorites. Wonder if Mom would bring my supper to my room? I mean, being grounded is like prison. I'm an outcast. Can't go anywhere; can't do anything.

Yeah, right. She doesn't feel *that* sorry for me.

I drag myself off the bed and down the stairs, moaning and feeling sorry for myself the whole way. By the time I get to the bottom, I ache in muscles that I bet my biology teacher doesn't know about. The spicy scent lures me to the kitchen, where a bowl of black bean spare ribs and a steaming platter of baby bok choy are on the table. My grandmother's standing at the stove, spooning rice into bowls.

"Your father's working late tonight," Mom says, as I slowly lower myself into the chair. She ignores my moans and rushes around, grabbing a serving spoon from the drawer and pouring a glass of milk for Kim. The phone rings. My mother answers it, as my grandmother brings two bowls of rice to the table.

"David," says my grandmother, as she hands Kim and me each a bowl. "Eat. You like this." Then she goes back to the stove to get rice for her and Mom.

The delicious smell of those golden brown ribs dotted with black beans, which normally draws me to the supper table without being called, barely stir my stomach. My social life is in the pits. What else could go wrong?

"What?!" my mom shrieks.

We all look at her. She's holding the phone to her ear, gripping the glass of milk and staring at my grandmother as if she's seen a ghost. "Who told you that?" she demands in Chinese.

Instinct tells me that something has gone horribly wrong. My mother, listening intently to the caller, suddenly fixes her eyes on me. Her face, which paled a few seconds ago, is now turning several shades of red. Almost as red as the lucky envelopes filled with money that Kim and I get from relatives at Chinese New Year.

Mom's still staring at me.

I don't feel so lucky.

"Somebody's in trouble," Kim sings softly, as she spoons some ribs and sauce into her rice bowl.

"Shut up," I mutter under my breath.

After thanking the caller, my mom hangs up the phone with a firm click. She sets Kim's glass of milk on the table with a solid thud.

"Who was that?" Nai-nai asks. She sits down at the table and picks up her chopsticks.

"Wong *Tai*," my mom answers. "She wanted to know how you are feeling."

Mrs. Wong has been playing mah-jongg with my grandmother for years. It's normal for old people to ask about their friends' health, isn't it?

"Strange that she would call just to ask that," says my grandmother.

"She called because Lim *Tai* told her that you were going to the hospital."

Ah! Mrs. Lim volunteers at the Chinese hospital. She probably just meant my grandmother was going to visit her. I grab the spoon and scoop up a helping of spare ribs.

"Hospital? Lim *Tai* has nothing to do but sit in her son's grocery store and talk," my grandmother replies.

Okay, it's normal for little old ladies to call each other to check on their health. It's a really nice thing to do. Friends looking after friends, like Craig and me.

My mom, staring straight at me, says to my grandmother, "Ng *Tai* told Lim *Tai* that her granddaughter will not go to the school dance with a boy because you are sick."

Kim stops eating and stares at me, wide-eyed. I can feel the blood draining from my face and flowing down to my feet.

"Don't chew with your mouth open," I say to Kim. She makes a face at me.

"Sick? I am not sick," my grandmother says in surprise. "Who would say such a thing?"

"David, do you know anything about this?" My mom's voice is firmly under control, which can be scarier than when she's yelling.

"I told Christine I can't take her to the grad."

"Did you tell her why?"

Why is it that even when mothers have it all figured out, they still torture you with petty details?

"No."

"*David.*" There's an edge of danger in her tone.

What does she want me to say? I'm in deep with Christine because she decided I had to be punished on top of being fired? I had to lie! Why can't she understand that?

"I can't tell her I can't go because I'm grounded because I got fired for stealing! She'll hate me!"

The phone rings. My grandmother gets up to answer it.

"David, I understand why you don't want Christine to know what happened," says Mom, "but telling lies won't help."

My grandmother's talking in Chinese, probably to another friend who heard the same rumor. "David, for you," she says.

Confused as to why one of my grandmother's friends wants to talk to me, I get up and take the phone. "Hello?"

"Your grandmother sounds pretty healthy to me!" Christine's angry voice blares out of the phone. I'm too stunned to reply.

Nai-nai's whispering to my mother.

"I can explain..."

"I don't care! You lied! Did you just change your mind about going with me?"

"No! I really want to go with you, but I can't. I'm grounded."

"For lying?"

"No, for stealing!" There's silence on the other end of the line. I wish I hadn't blurted it out like that.

"You're really something. I'm glad I'm not going to the grad with you anymore." The dial tone echoes her sentiment.

I didn't even get to explain. I don't know how I could have explained it, but I didn't even get the chance.

Christine can't possibly hate me as much as I hate myself right now.

CHAPTER 25

If I ever want proof that my parents are sentimental fools, all I have to do is come down to the basement. We moved into this house when I was just a few months old, and from the looks of it, my parents kept everything we ever owned. The layer of dust that covers the cardboard boxes, bags, and suitcases is proof that these haven't budged from the storeroom in years.

My parents thought it was time to clean it out, and since I'm grounded, they decided I was the best candidate to do it. I think they just wanted to get me out of my room. Mom and my grandmother have been cooking up my favorite snacks. The other night, when my dad brought home egg tarts as a treat, Kim let me have the last one. I must look really pathetic if my sister's being *that* nice to me.

Maybe they feel sorry for doing this to me. I saw my parents share a look. My dad raised his eyebrows at my mom, like he was asking her something, but she just sighed and turned away. They say actions speak louder than words. Right now, if they said, "You can go to the grad," it would be enough.

I can't study. The words in the textbooks don't make

any sense. Nothing sticks to my brain. I just keep reading the same line or paragraph over and over.

Christine is so mad at me. What can I say to make her forgive me? She snubbed me at school this morning. She walked past me and up the stairs like I wasn't there. I could barely concentrate on the Biology exam. Good thing it was multiple choice. Good thing I got good marks during the year. The final is only worth forty percent, so if I mess up, at least I'll still pass.

Normally, I hang around after exams to see how some of the others did, but everyone was talking about prom night. The news about Christine and me was all over the school in no time. People looked at their phones, and then looked at me in pity.

Someone sent Craig one of those text messages. His voice cracked as he said "Sorry" for the umpteenth time. But it wasn't really his fault, and I told him so, again and again. As for the girls, well, of course they sided with Christine. Not that I blame them. Everybody seemed as uncomfortable as I felt whenever the subject of the grad threatened to come up, so I didn't stick around.

Truth is, cleaning the basement makes me forget everything. Temporarily. And the mess down here is overwhelming. The only way to tackle it is to drag everything out and sort it. Clothing, books, household stuff, baby clothes, toys; there's more than enough for a garage sale. I grab the handle of a trunk and drag it out a few inches from the wall when something falls behind it with a harmonious plunk. I lean over the top of the trunk and peer into the gap. Reaching down, I wrap my hand around a slim, smooth surface and pull it up.

It's an acoustic guitar.

I carefully wipe the dust off with a rag, but a small cloud kicks up, making me sneeze. Putting my foot on top of the truck to hold the guitar in place, I pick at the strings and play a few notes. It needs a tune-up really badly, a little cleaning, and new strings. How lucky can a guy get! My parents said I'd have to wait before I can get another one, or earn the money on my own. But this dusty, scraped beauty is just what I need. I run my fingers down the neck, and one of the strings pops. No problem. I can fix it. Maybe I can keep it because I cleaned the basement.

The only question is, who does it belong to? My mom doesn't have any musical talent, and I know my dad doesn't appreciate rock 'n' roll. One time, I was sitting at my desk, looking over some chords Craig wrote. I was strumming and trying to fit words to the music, when I came up with the idea for *Burning' Rubber*. There was a noise in the hallway, and I yelled at Kim to stop spying on me. Then my dad stuck his head in the doorway and grinned.

Well, I don't care who this guitar belonged to; it's mine now. Finder's keepers.

It takes a couple of hours, but I manage to organize all this junk. I make piles of stuff for a garage sale, stuff for charity, stuff we can keep, and a couple of things for me, like that old Rolling Stones T-shirt. Where did that come from? Is it possible that my parents were cool?

My mom has had the same hairstyle since high school.

My dad can't coordinate his clothes by himself.

Nah. No way.

Someone's coming down the stairs. It's my mom, checking to see how I'm doing. Her arms are folded across her chest as if she doesn't know what to do with them. She looks pleased, even though she hasn't inspected my work yet. Ever since they grounded me, she's been pleased with anything and everything I do. Guilt does funny things to parents.

"How's it going?"

"There's so much junk!" I wave my arms over the family heirlooms that cover the floor. "Why'd you keep everything?"

Peeking into one of the cardboard boxes, she reaches inside and picks up the blue jacket I wore in kindergarten.

"It's just so hard to part with some things," she sighs. "Do you remember this?"

Oh, no. She's getting nostalgic over baby stuff. I roll my eyes. "Yeah. I was really upset that first day 'cause you left me there."

"I know." She giggles like I just told a joke. "You wouldn't talk to me when I came back to get you."

"I was traumatized," I say, in self-defense. "Child abandonment is an offence, you know." It happened over ten years ago, but I remember it like it was yesterday. She waved goodbye, and then disappeared out the classroom door. I bawled my eyes out until I realized all the other kids were staring at me. Embarrassed, the tears dried up pretty quick.

"But you couldn't wait to go back the next day."

"That's 'cause I liked playing with the electric train set." True. The teacher tried to make me feel better by showing me how to put the tracks together, and then letting me push the button to make the train run. It worked. When my mom came to pick me up, I cried because I didn't want to leave.

For the next half hour, my mom and I go over each pile, discussing what to keep and what to throw away. When she finds the box of baby toys, the stories about me get really silly.

Desperate to change the topic, I hold up the Rolling Stones T-shirt. "Who did this belong to?" It's black, faded, and just my size.

She looks at it with a squint, and then remembers. "Oh, it's George's. He stored some things here when he moved. I think that box of books is his, too."

Dad's older brother is a geek, a math genius and a partner in an accounting firm in Vancouver. The last time he and his wife visited us, my dad hinted pretty strongly that I should be an accountant. Accountants can always find a job, he said. Oh, yeah, like I plan to spend the rest of my life chained to a calculator.

"Can I keep it?"

"Sure. Wash it first." She turns and starts picking through the pile for charity.

"He likes the Stones?" I ball up the T-shirt and toss it on the stairs. "Uncle George thinks federal budgets are fun."

Mom laughs. "He was a teenager once, too, you know."

"Was this his, too? Can I keep it?" I hold up the guitar. The string that snapped is hanging off to the side.

Her eyes open in surprise, and she stares at it for a couple of seconds. For a moment, I'm afraid she'll say we have to send it back to Uncle George.

"Oh! Um… I suppose so." She hesitates, before adding with a little smile, "Oh, why not? Nobody's using it."

Yes! I score a T-shirt and a guitar. Things are looking up.

She looks through the rest of the stuff for a few more minutes, picking things up and tossing them onto other piles. When she's fed up and says we'll finish tomorrow, I grab the guitar and T-shirt and run up to my room.

Shutting the door behind me, I go over to my desk and lay the guitar on top, looking it over. The afternoon sunlight highlights the dust and dirt. If it was a Martin D-28, it'd be worth a lot of money, but there's no name on it. Considering that it's been in the basement for so long, I'm lucky it isn't warped. I open the bottom desk drawer, pull a cotton rag out of my cleaning kit, and wipe off the dust. It's all I can do. Maybe I'll ask Andrew if he has extra strings and can help me tune it.

I turn the posts and remove the pieces of broken string, then I pick up the guitar and gently play the scales on the remaining strings. It's off-key, but it's the best piece of music I've heard in awhile.

CHAPTER 26

"Hey, David!" Craig runs down the sidewalk towards me. He leaps over a puddle, almost dropping his backpack. It rained really hard last night. The air is damp and smells like wet grass. When Craig catches up, I hear strains of Green Day leaking out of his earbuds. We stick to the path instead of cutting across the muddy lawn, heading for the school's entrance.

"Hey, listen, I've been talking to the guys," Craig says, stuffing the earbuds into his pocket. "We're thinking of starting band practice next month."

"Seriously?" I ask, surprised but happy. "So you're not kicking me out?"

"No way!" Craig replies, looking surprised, and adds. "Andrew said he'll help you, if you want."

"Thanks. Yeah, that'd be great." Maybe they're asking because they feel sorry for me, but I don't care. I'm still in.

As we approach the school, I see Christine and Nathalie on the edge of the parking lot. Nathalie gives a little wave at Craig, and he does the same back.

Christine turns and looks at us. Then she makes a face as if someone just farted, and looks away. My insides crumble. The only thing keeping me up is that I don't want

Craig to see how much it hurts.

"Oh, man," Craig says, when he sees Christine's reaction.

I wish he'd stop doing that every time Christine ignores me. Okay, so I was ticked off at him when I got grounded. If he hadn't insisted that I put the money back, I wouldn't have gotten caught.

"I don't blame Christine for being mad at me," I say grudgingly. "Is she going with anyone?" I immediately regret asking. Knowing might be worse than not knowing. I don't want to picture some other guy dancing with her. Or doing anything else.

"Not according to Nathalie. Besides, grad's next week and it's kind of late to find a date."

True. The guys felt sorry for me when they found out. Even Bruno didn't know what to say. For all his wisdom in the ways of the world, he didn't have any advice on what I could say to Christine. I mean, these past few weeks we were almost like a couple. Sure, some kids are going in a group, and that's okay, but having a date means something. When a girl likes you enough to say yes, it gives a guy some swagger, some bragging rights.

If only I could talk to her. I don't know what I'd say, but if we're not going to the grad together, I'd feel better if she wasn't mad at me.

"So what're you gonna do?" Craig asks.

I shrug. "Think maybe I should find another job." I know that's not what he meant.

Craig nods. "Good idea."

Making a fresh start sounds good, but doesn't make me feel any better.

As we get closer to the school, the huge grad poster plastered to the doors catches my attention. I don't want to look at it, but I can't help it. The name "Queen Elizabeth Hotel" is in gold letters.

"Hey, they're coming this way," Craig says. Sure enough, Nathalie and Christine are heading towards the entrance. Nathalie slows down and looks at Craig. Then they look at me. It dawns on me that they colluded to give me the chance I was hoping for.

Christine's walking like she's determined to get past us as fast as possible. I step in front of her, as if by accident. She pretends not to notice, and takes a step sideways to go around me. I block her again.

"Move!" she blurts out, exasperated. She looks mad, but at least she's looking at me.

"Don't you want to know why I lied?"

"You already told me. It's because you stole something. You're a liar and a thief."

Even though her eyes are blazing, she looks hurt.

"I made a mistake," I say. "I took the money because things are tough at home." She rolls her eyes. "It's a lousy excuse, but that's why I did it. I was feeling sorry for myself." I swallow hard. "I'm an idiot."

She looks away, as if she's not listening. I tell her why I worked at Le Grenier de la musique for free. Christine glances at me.

I think I have a chance, and keep talking.

She looks concerned when I describe my bike accident. When I get to the part about how Mark caught me as I was putting the money back, there's a glimmer of sympathy in her eyes. The toughest part is coming up.

"I didn't want to disappoint you, and I didn't want you to hate me, so I made up that story about my grandmother."

There's a moment of silence. That's when I notice Craig and Nathalie have disappeared.

"If you'd told me the truth, I would have understood," Christine says softly.

"Sorry I ruined prom night for you."

"How is your grandmother, anyway?"

I groan. "She told all her friends what happened, and they're having a good laugh. Now I know who my sister takes after."

Christine giggles.

"You still gonna go?" I ask. My throat tightens up, afraid of her answer.

"Yeah," she says. "I'll meet the other girls there."

I'm torn between relief that nobody else has asked her and guilt that I let her down.

"What're you going to do?" she asks.

I shrug. "Well, I had to clean out the basement as part of my punishment, so maybe my parents will let me off for good behavior." I say it like a joke because it'll rain soy sauce before that happens.

Christine nods. "That would be nice," she says.

"Yeah, it would."

"It would also be nice if we did something after the grad dance," she adds.

"Seriously?"

"Yeah. Something that doesn't cost anything," she says. "There's an old saying, you know, 'The best things in life are free.'" And she gives me that smile.

CHAPTER 27

It took another few days, but the basement looks a heck of a lot better now. Mom's excited because there's a pile of stuff for a garage sale: old furniture, books, toys, and useless stuff. If it's nice next weekend, we'll set up a couple of tables in the driveway. Maybe she'll let me keep the money for doing all the work. Doubt it, though. The money will come in handy to pay the bills.

Her "inspections" didn't fool me. She was checking to see if there was anything she wanted to keep. She couldn't part with the artwork Kim and I had made for Mother's Day, Valentine's Day, and every other holiday in the calendar year. Then my sister and grandmother got into the act. Kim wanted to keep all of her toys for a rainy day. My grandmother saw potential use for everything else. Yeah, like if there's ever a tornado coming, we can strap down the furniture with the balls of string she wanted to keep.

It could've been worse, but I got upset and put my foot down. There was some grumbling, but hey, I'm the one who put in all the hours and sweat. I don't want to have to do it all over again.

They came to their senses. Compromises were made.

The string won't find any sanctuary here.

My mom's happy, and since she hasn't said anything else about doing more work around the house, I'm not going to either. I kind of want to ask if I can go to the prom, but I can't. We haven't talked about it since the day I got fired. It's the elephant in the room nobody talks about. So I have to keep busy, especially tonight.

Because it's prom night, and I don't want to think about what I'm missing.

Sure, it's a big night. Graduating from high school's a big deal, but grad's only one night in my lifetime. I have a future to look forward to, goals to accomplish. It's just a big party that all my friends and Christine are going to.

I wonder if she'll miss me.

Man, this is depressing. Snap out of it.

First thing to do is fix the guitar. It's starting to look good, after just a little bit of cleaning. Shutting myself in my room, I grab my backpack and pull out the strings and winder Andrew gave me, then get to work.

During one of my lessons at Le Grenier de la musique, Mark showed me how to change the strings. I find my notebook, flip through the pages to the instructions, and read them a couple of times to jog my memory.

I'm going to practice every day. Maybe we'll get some gigs at schools, play small clubs, and who knows? We might get a following.

Pumping Iron, one night only!

Then we'll cut our own CD. Yeah. Play some cover songs, and Craig and I'll write our own.

I need to find a job for the summer. A paying job this time. With my own money, I'll be able to take guitar lessons again, get a cell phone, and maybe even get a nice set of second-hand wheels.

I'm done, and it looks good. I pick at a few strings. The guitar feels good in my hands, but it sounds a bit off. I adjust the keys and play again. It still doesn't sound right.

My old desktop computer grunts as it powers up. Then

I click on Google and search the internet for an online guitar tuner. I find one, and turn up the speakers. It takes me awhile to tune the guitar. Maybe I'll ask Andrew if he has a tuner, just to be sure.

Since I'm on the internet, I should check out Jobboom.com.

What kind of job could I do? Wonder if anyone will ask about Le Grenier de la musique. Maybe it's better not to mention I worked there. Lu Bin once told me I could always work at the grocery store, but I don't want to work with my dad. He still goes out most nights and comes back after midnight. I don't want to know where he's been or who he's been with. There's no way he's working at the grocery store that late, and he always comes back before Mom's shift is over.

Mom'll never find out as long as I don't bring it up.

There's openings for sales clerks, cashiers, short-order cooks, call centers. Maybe software companies are looking for video game testers? I type in "video game tester" in the search engine. Nothing.

If only I wasn't so stupid, I'd be getting ready to pick up Christine for the prom right about now. If only dad didn't blow so much money at the gambling table. How much money do those guys make playing guitar in the metro? My parents would freak if I did that. They'd think it's begging.

There's a faint knock on the door. Kim's standing in the doorway. "Wanna play *Mario* with me?"

"No."

"What're you doing?"

"None of your business."

"Looking for another job?"

How the heck did she know? "No! Why don't you go bother Dad?"

"'Cause he's going out."

"Again?"

She nods.

"Where's he going?"

She shrugs.

"You don't know? You know I'm looking for a job, but you don't know where Dad's going?"

"I guessed," she grins proudly. "You keep falling for it."

"Well, then guess where Dad's going."

"Someplace new," Kim says teasingly.

"What do you mean?"

"I mean, someplace he's never been before."

"How do you know that?"

"Why should I tell you?"

For once, I'm prepared to play her little game. "Because you want to."

"No, I don't," she says firmly.

I pull open the bottom desk drawer and pull out my secret weapon. Fuzzy, the floppy pink rabbit she loved when she was little. She screamed and cried when she lost it years ago, but I found it in the basement stuck between some boxes, where it's been hiding all these years. It's not so fuzzy anymore. It's dirty and dusty, but her eyes bug out when she sees it.

"Fuzzy!" she screams, and runs over to grab it out of my hands.

But I'm quicker and taller than she is. I stand up, holding the toy over my head with one hand. "Tell me, or you'll never see Fuzzy again."

Instantly, she stops, pouts, and folds her arms across her chest. "I don't care," she says, keeping an eye on her beloved Fuzzy.

"Yes, you do," I say threateningly. "I found him, and I can make Fuzzy disappear for good."

"No!"

"Where's Dad going?"

"I don't know!"

"Guess!"

She scrunches up her face. "Someplace fancy," she

finally says, her face lighting up in realization. "He was polishing his shoes."

Polishing his shoes? He wears an old pair of Nikes to work.

"Where's Mom?" I ask.

"Work."

I drop the ragged bunny on the floor and race out of my room.

The door to my parents' room is closed. I put my ear against the door, and listen. The faint sound of running water confirms my dad's in the shower. Slowly turning the handle, I open the door a few inches, just enough to take a look inside. On the bed is a black pair of pants and a white tuxedo jacket. The shiny black shoes are on the floor.

Kim, cradling the sorry-looking Fuzzy in her arms, pushes me aside to take a peek. "Where do you think he's going?"

Not to work, but I don't say that.

The sound of running water stops. I push Kim back, and quietly close the door. Kim follows me back to my room.

"Do you know where's he's going?" she asks again.

"No," I say. But I'm afraid of who he's going with.

CHAPTER 28

Everybody needs a friend they can count on. Craig is mine.

He was getting ready to pick up Nathalie, when I phoned and told him what was going on and the crazy idea I had. He said he and Nathalie would get here as fast as they could.

I kept an eye on Kim to make sure she didn't say anything to Dad, but she didn't budge from my side, either because she wanted to know what I was up to or because she was afraid of what Dad was up to.

Now we're both sitting on the sofa in the living room with my grandmother watching a Chinese variety show. The contortionists are doing amazing tricks with dishes and sticks, but the only thing I'm paying attention to is the sound of my dad's movements upstairs. What if he leaves before Craig gets here? What am I going to do if Craig gets here before my dad leaves?

Kim is attuned to every move I make. When I get up to look out the window for Craig's car, she's right beside me.

"What're we looking for?" she asks, still clutching Fuzzy. She eagerly looks up and down the street, but there's nothing unusual, just the same old cars, dogs, and kids.

"Nothing," I say, wondering if Craig parked somewhere down the block to keep out of sight. I can't leave before my dad does.

I hear his footsteps on the stairs. I run back to the sofa with Kim on my heels, and we throw ourselves onto the cushions, pretending to be absorbed in the show. Stupid, I know, since it's not a crime to look out the window, but I'm nervous and don't want to give anything away.

I hear him behind us, and turn around. He's dressed as if he's going on a date.

I feel sick.

"You look pretty, Daddy. Where are you going?" Kim asks. For once, I'm glad she's nosy.

"Thank you, Kim. I have to go out," he replies. "You be a good girl and look after your grandmother."

"Out where?" I demand.

He looks surprised by my question. "I have some work to do," he says.

"You moving boxes dressed like that?" I stare at him, defying him to lie to my face. Does he really think I believe him?

"No," he says, in that tone that tells me the subject is closed. Then he says goodbye to my grandmother, opens the front door, and leaves.

Kim and I race to the window in time to see him get into the car and back out of the driveway.

Where's Craig? I desperately scan the parked cars. Then I see it. The Mazda is inching out from behind the hedges of a neighbor's driveway across the street.

"I'm going out!" I shout out to my grandmother in Chinese, and run out the door before she has a chance to ask where.

I get to the curb just as Craig and Nathalie pull up. "Don't lose him!" I yell, and open the back door. Kim tries to jump in ahead of me, but I grab her and shove her out of the way. She stumbles backwards, but doesn't fall. "You can't come."

"You're not supposed to go out!" Kim cries. She grips Fuzzy by the ear and dangles him close to the ground.

"No, I'm just not allowed to go to the grad!" I jump into the back seat and slam the door shut. "Let's go!" I say to Craig, and snap on my seatbelt. The tires screech as we take off.

A block away, Dad's car pauses at the stop sign.

"Don't get too close," I instruct Craig, when he stops at the corner.

"Don't worry," Craig replies. "He doesn't know my car."

"How're you doing, David?" Nathalie asks.

"Hey, Nat. Okay, I guess." Then I notice that she's all dressed up and looking very pretty. "Sorry to ruin your plans, but I can't do this alone."

"It's okay," she says, and gives me a look that tells me it really is. "Craig explained it to me." There's a pause before she quietly adds, "My parents are getting a divorce."

I nod in sympathy because I can't speak. My throat tightens up with gratitude for my two friends.

We turn onto the boulevard and follow my dad, hiding one or two cars behind, but keeping him in sight. After awhile, it becomes clear that he's heading downtown.

"Where do you think he's going?" Craig asks, as we follow him onto the highway up-ramp.

"I don't know," I say, fighting to keep images of him and that woman out of my mind.

Once we're on the highway heading for the Champlain Bridge, it's easy to keep him in sight. Although it's late in the afternoon, the sky's clear and the sun's bright. Now we're right behind him, but since there's not a lot of traffic, Craig stays back a distance, just to be safe.

My stomach's tied up in knots. There's no thrill to this chase. It's not like in the movies, where the good guy trails the bad guy to find the answer to a mystery or a secret location. My dad's not a bad guy; he just made a couple of mistakes. But if I don't stop him, he'll do something he'll regret for the rest of his life. I don't know what I'm going to say when I catch up to him. It's not like I'm going to read him his rights.

A dirty white delivery van cuts in front of us. "Move it!" I say to the van in frustration.

"Don't worry," Craig says calmly. "We won't lose him."

When my dad stops at the red light at the end of the highway, I'm grateful the van's between us, but I have to control the urge to poke my head out the window to make sure he's still there.

"Listen," I say. "When he gets out of the car, just let me out so I can follow him. You guys can go to the grad."

"We're going with you," Craig says firmly. "You might need backup. And we were going downtown anyway."

Nathalie agrees. "It's no big deal if we're late. Besides, according to the directions my dad gave me, we're not far from the hotel."

I duck my head down, so they don't see what it means to me. To tell the truth, I'm relieved not to be doing this alone.

The highway ends at a boulevard where a cluster of towering office buildings guards the downtown entrance like a bouncer at a club. Merging traffic, with cars cutting in and out of lanes, slows us down.

"Don't lose him," I say, as Craig slaps the steering wheel in frustration.

We're a few cars behind him in the center lane when my dad veers to the left. Craig swears because the other drivers won't let us in. If we stay in this lane and move up, we'll end up right beside him. There's an impatient honk behind us.

"Oh, shut up!" Nathalie replies to a long blare.

"You can't turn left in this lane," I say, feeling desperate and trying not to lose hope.

"Oh, yeah?" Craig replies.

We sit helplessly at the red light and watch as the cars beside us get the green to turn left. My dad's car slowly moves around the corner.

"Come on, come on," Craig mutters to the traffic light. Miraculously, it turns green. When we get to the intersection, Craig burns rubber turning left and cuts off a car that was too slow to react. There's an angry honk and I think maybe a fist, but Craig makes it around the corner and down the street just in time for us to see my dad's car enter an underground parking lot. Craig floors it. The seatbelt keeps me from being thrown to the other side of the car, as we take a sharp right turn with tires screeching.

"Where are we?" Nathalie asks. Good question. There's nothing but loading docks and garage entrances on this short street. He really got dressed up to unload boxes?

"How am I going to follow him in here?" I ask, as we pull up to the entrance. "I can't get into the elevator with him, and he knows Craig." Craig punches the button on the machine, and it spits out a ticket. I look at it hoping to find out where we are, but a numbered company welcomes us to their underground parking lot. The automatic arm rises, and we enter. Craig carefully drives down the concrete ramp. At the bottom, we see the car turning in at the end of an aisle.

"Your dad doesn't know me," Nathalie says. "I can follow him and text Craig." She opens her purse, pulls out her phone, and turns it on. A small can tumbles out, and Craig catches it with his right hand before it falls between the seats. He glances at it.

"Pepper spray?" he asks in disbelief. "Why are you carrying this?"

Nathalie sighs. "My dad gave it to me. He wants to be sure I'm safe."

"Oh, man!" Craig shakes his head in disbelief.

"I'm not going to use it on you, silly," she laughs, and takes the can and puts it back into her purse, along with the phone.

"Oh."

How are we going to park without him seeing us? We follow him deeper into the garage, spiraling down to the next level. Then my dad pulls into a spot. I duck down as we pass by, and after we round the next corner, Nathalie gets out of the car and heads to the elevator. I peek out the window and see my dad heading in the same direction. He looks like a different person: hair slicked back, looking excited and dressed up for a party. I've never seen him like that, and he looks good. I think I can see why my mom fell for him, and it makes me sad. I lose sight of him and Nathalie as we continue down to the next parking level.

Craig pulls into the first empty spot. We're heading to the elevators when I suddenly realize we have to take the stairs.

"Why?" Craig protests. "You know how far down we are?"

"Well, what if they end up getting on the same elevator as us?"

"Right," he says, and we push open the door to the stairwell, take the steps two at a time.

"Did she call yet?" I ask, when we reach the next level up.

Craig pulls his phone from the inside pocket of his jacket. "Can't get a signal here."

We hurry up the stairs. By the time we reach the door marked "Rez-de-chaussée," we're both a bit out of breath. The ding of an arriving elevator sends us back into the stairwell and behind the door. We open the door a crack, and are relieved to see an elderly couple get off. Then we follow them up the escalator to the lobby.

Whatever this place is, it looks expensive and intimidating enough to make us speak in whispers without being told. Overgrown chandeliers throw light on the patterned wall-to-wall carpeting. The lobby is humongous, scattered with leather chairs and sofas. People, some pulling suitcases, are dressed in business suits or jeans.

They walk by clothing boutiques, a souvenir store, and a restaurant with white tablecloths and candles.

It's weird, but I have a feeling I've been here before.

Craig checks his phone again. "She's sent a message. She says to go to the mezzanine level. We won't believe where we are."

"Let's go," I say, and look around for a sign to point the way.

"Hey," Craig says. He points to a couple of people at the other side of the room, a guy in a dark suit and a girl in a gown who are walking away from us. "Isn't that Bruno?"

"Looks like him," I say, "but it can't be."

Come to think of it, there are a lot of kids our age, all dressed up. A few more people walk by us, when I catch a glimpse of her face. I signal Craig to stop.

"That's her," I whisper, motioning to the girl in the red dress heading towards the stairs. "The girl we saw my dad with." Up close, I can see she's really young, too young for my dad. And pretty. How could he hurt my mother this way? And me and Kim?

We follow her at a safe distance, but she doesn't go far. According to the sign, she's heading to the mezzanine level. Up there, a big crowd is all dressed up, as if…

As if they're going to a prom!

The Asian Jennifer Lopez walks right past Bruno and his date. They're talking to Andrew and Francine. There are a couple of kids from my Biology class. What the…

What the heck is the matter with my dad?

He's taking *that* girl to my grad!

CHAPTER 29

Nothing makes sense. I collapse onto the closest chair in shock. My dad's going to humiliate me in front of all my friends. Life as I know it is over.

I'll have to change my name, move to another city, or become a hermit.

"What's your dad doing here?" Craig asks, as he scans the crowd. "And where is he?" He pulls out his phone and types into the keyboard. "I'm telling Nathalie where we are." He pauses and looks at the screen. "Okay," he says. "She's coming to get us."

A couple of students walking by say "hi" to Craig and stare at me, or more likely my jeans, sneakers, and the black Rolling Stones T-shirt. I'm a loser who doesn't know how to dress for prom. Right now, I don't care.

Nathalie comes running up to us with a big smile on her face. "David, you have to come see this."

"I don't know if I can take any more surprises." I don't want to get out of the chair. This is all a mistake. I shouldn't have followed him. This is turning out to be a bigger nightmare than I thought.

She takes my hand in both of hers and tugs. "Come on. Trust me. It's okay."

I let her pull me up. Craig and I follow her through the crowd of excited students hanging around the double doors to the ballroom.

"David! You made it after all," Elaine exclaims, as she checks tickets at the door. "Cool outfit. Very daring."

"Thanks. I could say the same for you." Her gown, made of feathers and ribbons, is an eyeful, but it's pure Elaine. I hope her date doesn't have any allergies. I stick my hands in my back pockets. "Uh, I forgot my ticket. I wasn't sure I was coming."

Elaine waves me in. "No problem. I know you have one." Craig and Nathalie show their tickets, and then we open the double doors and enter. When we emerge on the other side, it's as if we're in a different universe. When the grad committee checked out the ballroom a few weeks ago, it was just a big, empty room with a high ceiling and humongous chandeliers. Now the same room is dressed with balloons, banners, white tablecloths, fancy place settings, and centerpieces. It looks like a scene out of a movie. Waiters are walking around with trays of hors d'oeuvres. It's as if I crashed some high-society party.

Miss Shrilly is standing near the alcohol-free bar, chatting with a couple of teachers. People are wandering around the room searching for their table. Some are on the dance floor. The music is loud and hot. I can't make out anybody's face in the dim lighting. A part of me is hoping my dad changed his mind and didn't come.

"Where is he?" I ask Nathalie.

She points towards the dance floor.

I close my eyes, unwilling to stand here and watch as my father makes a fool of himself with some girl half his age. My chest heaves as I struggle to breathe. I open my eyes and peer at the dark figures on the floor. Nathalie puts her arm around my shoulder and puts her lips close to my ear. "Not out there, on the stage."

Blinking to adjust to the stage lights, I see the band. A woman who looks a lot like Tiffany at the Kowloon

Supermarket is singing into the microphone. After a couple of seconds, I realize it really is her. The power and beauty of her voice surprises me.

And standing next to her playing the guitar is... My dad!

"Dad?" My mind struggles with the idea that the guitarist on stage could be him. Is him.

Tiffany ends the song with a flourish. Is that Sammy Chin on the drums? I recognize the beat he pounded on the boxes in the grocery store. My dad plays the first few notes of the next song, and the band follows his lead. The other men, who I finally realize are Kien, Tom, and Peng, are dressed in white dinner jackets, red ties, and black pants, just like my dad. A woman in a red dress steps onto the stage and up to the microphone. My mouth drops open when I recognize her. The Asian Jennifer Lopez sounds great.

"Isn't this amazing?" Nathalie shouts above the music.

Craig looks as stunned as I am. "When did your dad learn how to play guitar?"

"I don't know. He never told me he could."

"Nathalie!" a voice behind us calls out. It's Christine. She looks beautiful in a jade green strapless gown. Simplicity on any other girl would have been plain. She and Nathalie compliment each other on their dresses, but Christine smiles at me, and right now, I don't care if I look like a loser because she doesn't think I am.

"You came?" says Christine.

I nod. "I owe you an explanation. It's kind of hard, but..."

"Did you come to see your dad?" She gestures towards the stage, where my dad's playing a rocking solo and looking pretty cool.

"Yeah, but I didn't know he was here." Maybe I should shut up before I put my foot in my mouth. "It's a long story."

"Want to dance?" Christine asks shyly, as if I might say

no.

But she has just made my dream come true. I hold out my arm and escort her to the dance floor, just like my mom showed me.

It's hard to resist the band's beat. We find a spot on the floor and join the rocking motion of elbows, hips, and feet. I have to admit my dad's pretty good at fingering the strings as lead guitarist. Nobody else knows that he's my dad. They're just the band playing at our grad dance, and damn, they're good. I don't know what to think or feel. My emotions are a mix of pride, resentment for what he put the family through, and irritation that he kept the band a secret.

He has some explaining to do.

After a couple of songs, they take a break. I escort Christine back to her table.

"Are you mad at me?" I ask her. This is dangerous territory, but I've been there before and survived. Besides, I don't get what's going on.

She tilts her head as if she's thinking about it. "You mean for showing up here even after you told me twice your parents wouldn't let you come?"

I nod.

"I saw your dad before, and he told me why they busted you." She gives me a smile that tells me everything really is okay. "You made a mistake, David. You made a bad choice, but I don't think you have the heart to be a thief."

Out of relief, out of pure emotion and gratitude, I hug her, tight, and she hugs me back.

"I'll be back," I say.

"It's okay, David. Go talk to your dad."

I make my way to the stage. Sammy's sitting off to the side, mopping his brow and sipping a glass of water.

"Hey, David," Sammy says, in a heavy Chinese accent. "Congratulations. You graduate now." We shake hands.

"Thanks," I say. "And you guys sound great. So how

long have you been playing together?"

"A few months. At first, we played after work in the storage room just for fun. I used to bang on the boxes to drive Lu Bin crazy." He shakes with mischievous laughter. "And we were good! Then a few weeks ago, your dad suggested we play for real. He never told you?"

I shake my head. "Where is he?" Sammy cocks his head towards the doors. I say "bye" to him and push open the ballroom door, which leads to a carpeted corridor.

My dad's on the other side, talking to Kien and Tom. I take a slow, deep breath. What am I going to say?

"...so the banquet manager asked if we'd be interested in playing a Chinese wedding next month," my dad tells them. "The pay seems pretty good."

"Sounds good to me," Tom replies.

Kien sees me standing behind my dad. "David! So you came to hear the old man play, eh?"

My dad spins around. Shades of emotions cross his face: surprise, confusion, embarrassment, and pride, but not anger.

"Hey," I say, trying to sound casual. "You guys sounded pretty good up there."

"Thanks, David," Tom says, with a big smile. "Your dad says you're learning guitar. Maybe someday you can play with us."

He's actually telling people I'm learning guitar?

"Yeah, sure," I say, trying to keep the sound of surprise from my voice. "When I get better at it."

Kien frowns. "You wore jeans to the grad? Is that what kids do nowadays?"

Embarrassed, I touch my T-shirt. It doesn't matter if they're rock 'n' roll royalty, a Rolling Stones T-shirt just isn't prom wear. "Uh, I was in a hurry and didn't have time to change."

Kien raises an eyebrow and glances at my dad, who shrugs uncomfortably. After a nanosecond of silence, he and Tom nod politely, as if they understand. "We should tell Tiffany and the guys. See you later," Kien says, backing away. He must sense the awkwardness between me and my dad, and motions for Tom to follow him back to the ballroom.

I lean against the wall. My dad and I stand silently side-by-side for a few moments, without looking at each other. After the doors close behind Tom and Kien, I say what's on my mind.

"Why didn't you tell me?" I'm not angry, anxious, embarrassed, or any of the other emotions that drove me to follow him down here in the first place; what I am is confused.

My dad looks at the glass in his hand as if the answer is etched in the ice cubes. "It was supposed to be a surprise. Sort of like a graduation present."

"The surprise part worked."

"Good." But he doesn't sound pleased.

"Grad present, huh? Would've been nice if I was allowed to see it."

"That's your mother's fault," he says, sounding defensive. "I told her she went overboard with the punishment, but she felt she couldn't take it back."

The memories of what started it all in the first place stir up guilty feelings, so I change the topic. "So Mom knows you're here?"

"Of course. We've talked about this since… Well, since I had to look for a second job." He twists his mouth and looks sad. "I know I let the family down. I really…" He pauses, "I screwed up."

"So did I," I say sheepishly. "Like father, like son."

He smirks, and shakes his head.

"But you know," I say, "I don't understand something."

"What?"

"If you don't want me to play the guitar, why are you doing it?"

"I'm not against you playing the guitar. It's just not a

stable career," he says. "Your grandfather gave me a hard time about it, too."

"He wanted you to be an accountant?" I ask, reminding him of his choice of careers for me.

My dad laughs. "Okay, I get it. It's not for you either." Then he gets serious. "Your grandfather didn't want me to spend my life in a hand laundry, like he did," he says. "He had a hard life and wanted more for me." He pauses. "And it's something I want for you. It's what every father wants for their children.

"One of my friends had a band, and we played in clubs. We made money, but not a lot. Then I met your mom." He smiles at the memory. "After we got married, we talked about starting a family." He pauses and shakes his head. "I had to give it up. The band had enough gigs for me to pay the rent, but not enough to raise children. I found a job at the clothing factory, and never looked back."

"So why are you playing now?"

"That's your fault."

"Me? I didn't do anything. I didn't even know you played."

"You have something I didn't have," he says, "passion and talent."

"Talent?" I ask, surprised.

"Better than me," he says proudly. "I thought you could learn from my mistakes. Instead, I learned something from you."

"What's that?"

"Not to give up. Just because I'm not going to be a huge success at it doesn't mean that I can't do it at all."

"And don't you forget that," I say half-jokingly. I glance down at my feet, ashamed of what I had suspected him of doing. Which reminds me. "Who's that other girl?"

"Mei Mei. She's in the church choir with Tiffany. We wanted to expand our repertoire and thought a second singer would bring another dimension to the band. She's pretty good." Then he adds, "She was trying out for the band that night you saw me on Sainte-Catherine Street. And for your information," he says, wagging a finger at me, "you should be grateful I didn't tell your mother you snuck out that night."

I nod, agreeing, thinking that it was a good thing *I* didn't tell my mom. It's hard to wrap my mind around this whole scenario. My dad, who never even listens to music, plays in a band at night to earn extra money. How crazy is that?

"So you've been playing clubs?" I ask.

He shrugs. "Just a couple, and Lu Bin booked us for some private parties in Chinatown. The pay's not bad, and it's fun to play with the guys." He pauses and grins. "You know how it is."

That, I do.

"I saw Christine before," he says.

"She told me."

"You know, I first met your mother at her grad," he says. "I didn't go to her school, but I was playing in the band that night. A lot of girls hung around in between sets, but your mother, she was unforgettable. But she had a boyfriend. We didn't meet again until years later. I was visiting a friend at the hospital and your mom was the nurse looking after him."

"You picked her up?" I tease. "Dad, I don't think I'm old enough to hear the rest."

He smirks. "Maybe not." Then he adds, "By the way, how do you like my old guitar?"

"What?" I practically choke. "It was yours?"

He laughs and nods. "It's an old no-name brand, but I learned how to play with it. I forgot it was in the basement." Then he pauses. "So you're not embarrassed to have your messed-up old man play at your grad?"

"Are you kidding? Get back in there, and show me what you can do."

And he does.

CHAPTER 30

After looking around the ballroom, I see Christine out dancing with some of her friends. Everyone's having a good time, and word gets around that it's my dad's band. A few kids give me a thumbs-up.

Christine and I lock eyes with each other as I push my way through the dancers. When I get close, I whisper in her ear, "Want to see something special?"

She nods.

I take her hand, and lead her out of the ballroom.

* * *

"Sorry," says the desk clerk, with an apologetic look. "The room isn't occupied, but it's late. We don't want to disturb the other guests."

"Okay, thanks," I say, disappointed. Christine and I turn away from the reception desk and cross the lobby to head back to the grad.

"It was a good idea," Christine says, trying to console me. "Just bad timing."

"I have a lot of that lately," I reply. "But what if we went up anyway?"

A mischievous look crosses her face. "Let's go." She grabs my hand and pulls me towards the elevators.

* * *

The doors slide open on the seventeenth floor, and we step out. The hallway is empty and quiet. Christine points at the sign. We turn a corner, and follow the arrow to the end of a short corridor to Suite 1742, a piece of music history. A brass plate on the door reads "The John Lennon, Yoko Ono Suite."

"This is it," I tell Christine. "This is where they recorded *Give Peace a Chance*."

"I don't think I know that song," Christine says, with a frown.

"You hear it a lot at Christmas," I say. "They stayed in bed to protest for peace and called it a 'bed-in.'" I try the door handle. "Wonder if my mom'll buy that the next time I sleep in?"

Christine giggles.

The door's locked. No surprise there.

"Hey, wait. I want a picture." Christine pulls out her cell phone. She takes a photo of me standing beside the sign on the door, and I do the same for her. Pretty soon, we're goofing around, taking silly pictures of ourselves.

The quiet ding of an elevator arriving interrupts our fun. Christine guiltily puts away her phone. "What if it's a security guard? He might think we're trying to break in."

There's no escape route. The elevators are between us and the stairs at the other end of the hall.

"Okay," I whisper, as I grab her hand. "Change of plan. Let's just pretend we belong. How would anyone know?"

"Do we look like we can afford to stay in this hotel?" she giggles.

We dissolve into a fit of nervous laughter at that crazy notion, and bump into each other, making us laugh even more. I don't know if it's the sound of approaching footsteps and quiet voices that makes me giddy, or just being here with Christine. I look at her, and she looks at me. I'm glad she's here. It makes me want to…

Kiss her.

Someone taps my shoulder, and that's when I realize Christine and I are standing there, our arms wrapped around each other, lip-locked.

"Hey," says a familiar voice. "Get a room."

I reluctantly release Christine and turn around. Craig has a big smirk across his face. Nathalie's beside him, her hand covering a giggle.

"What are you doing up here?" I ask Craig.

"Not what you're doing," he says teasingly.

"You wish," I shoot back. Nathalie's face turns beet red. I think I'm close to the truth.

"Nat's aunt is showing us John Lennon's room," Craig says, thumbing towards the suite. That's when I notice a woman in a hotel uniform, her hair and eyes the same color as Nathalie's, standing at the open door. "Wanna see it?"

"Sure," Christine and I eagerly reply.

The moment we enter, I'm in awe.

We step into the foyer. Two sets of French doors are on the opposite wall, a kitchenette on the right and a bathroom on the left.

"There he is!" Craig points excitedly at a black-and-white photo of John Lennon hanging on the wall between the French doors. We rush over to look at it, and photos of John and Yoko in bed on another wall.

"Wow," is all any of us can say. I gently touch the photo with my fingertips, as if I can reach back in time.

"You should read this." Nathalie's aunt points to a picture frame hanging beside the bathroom. "It's an article about the bed-in." We huddle together, silently reading about what happened that day in 1969.

Then Nat's aunt opens one of the French doors, and

we follow her in. It's a living room with plump chairs, luxurious carpeting, end-table lamps, huge windows, and another set of glass doors to one side. Considering it's a hotel, all the suites are probably decorated the same way, except this one has gold records of *Give Peace a Chance* in a huge picture frame.

But it's the bedroom we want to see.

"Are you ready for this?" Nat's aunt asks. Then she flings open the double doors. "Ta-da!"

And we see it.

The king-size bed is covered with a white duvet and pillows. More framed pictures of the bed-in hang on the walls. We cluster in the doorway, afraid to step into the sacred space.

"Wow," Nathalie says in wonder. "That's the bed where it happened?"

"Not exactly," her aunt says, with a laugh. "It happened over forty years ago. I'm pretty sure they've changed the bed since then."

"I saw it on a television show about the sixties," I say. "All kinds of people were in the room. They sat around the bed, and sang, and played guitar."

"Did you know that John Lennon dragged the mattress from the bedroom to the living room?" Nathalie's aunt asks. "That why in all the pictures, you see the mattress in front of the windows in the living room."

"Cool," Craig says, in awe.

Then Nathalie's aunt looks at us with a mischievous smile and asks, "Do you want to sit on the bed?"

In response, we scream and dash and dive on the bed, laughing as we scramble for a spot in history. Christine hands Nathalie's aunt her cell phone, and we pose for pictures for posterity. Soon the girls and Nathalie's aunt are exploring the rest of the suite, while Craig and I stretch out on the king-sized bed.

"Wow," Craig whispers. We're looking at the pictures of John and Yoko on the wall. I wonder if he is as affected by the energy in the suite as I am; to be in the hotel room where one of our heroes wrote and recorded one of the most famous songs in the world.

"Hey, David," says Craig. "You know, maybe you can ask your dad for some pointers."

I think about this for a minute, remembering my conversation with my dad. "It might be better for me to take lessons, you know, do it my way. Besides," I say proudly, "I think my dad's going to be busy nights and weekends."

"Good idea," says Craig. Then he pauses and says, "He's good, you know."

"Yeah," I say proudly. "He is."

* * *

Nathalie's aunt has to get back to work, so after we fix up the bed, we take the elevator and head back to the prom.

There's a party going on! I can't believe how loud the music is, considering that at home my dad barely turns the radio above a conversational level. Now he's doing a rockabilly rhythm 'n' blues tune that's driving everybody wild. Even the teachers can't resist. Miss Shrilly's making moves on the dance floor that are impressive.

This is the craziest night of my life. My dad—the most boring, predictable human being in the world—is on stage, making this prom come alive with the most amazing music. Why didn't I know about this before? How could I have been so wrong about him?

What else don't I know about him?

"Come on," Christine says. She grabs my hand and pulls me into the crowd. We elbow and squeeze our way beside Bruno and his date. The floor's packed, but that's okay; it just makes Christine and me a lot closer. Neither one of us is complaining. The band plays a medley of Beatles songs, and when they finish, the room explodes into whistles and applause.

Especially from me.

"And now we have a special treat for you," Dad announces. "We're going to play a song written by two very talented people who are friends of yours, Craig Chemielewski and my son, David Chang. It's called *Burning Rubber.*"

What?

"And," continues my dad, "I'd like to invite them to play with us on stage."

"Yeah!" says Craig, pumping his fist in the air. "David, come on! Let's go!"

"I don't know," I say. The memory of the fiasco at the Montreal Rocks Contest still haunts me. It took awhile before the taunts over the YouTube video died down, and I don't want to do anything to remind the entire graduating class of that day.

"It's your song. You know it better than anyone," Craig says, putting his hand on my shoulder for reassurance. "It'll be okay." Cheers demanding our presence grow louder as I watch him dive into the crowd, making his way towards the stage.

"You can do it," says Christine. She kisses me for encouragement.

It works.

Next thing I know, I'm on stage. Craig's sitting behind the drums, ready and waiting. It's scary and thrilling at the same time. The crowd is chanting our names.

I look around for a guitar. The guys in the band are smiling at me, but nobody's making a move. Then my dad walks over with a strange smile on his face.

He lifts the strap over his head, hands me his guitar, and says, "You're the lead."

ABOUT THE AUTHOR

Day's Lee was born and raised in Montreal, Canada. Her desire to be a writer began in elementary school and led her to study journalism at Concordia University. As a freelance writer, she published articles in local and national magazines. Her first book, a children's picture book entitled *The Fragrant Garden* was published by Napoleon Publishing in 2005. Visit her website at www.dayslee.ca.

CPSIA information can be obtained at www.ICGtesting.com
Printed in the USA
LVOW10s0841050415

433215LV00015B/140/P